Murder
in the
Highlands

A Lady Marjorie Snellthorpe Mystery
Book 2

Dawn Brookes

Murder
in the
Highlands

A Lady Marjorie Snellthorpe Mystery

Dawn Brookes

Oakwood Publishing

Paperback Edition 2022
Paperback ISBN: 978-1-913065-59-1
Copyright © DAWN BROOKES 2022
Cover Images adapted from Adobe Stock Images:
Scottish Highlands
Elderly lady in foreground
Cover Design: John and Janet

Chapter 1

Lady Marjorie Snellthorpe could hear her cousin-in-law huffing and puffing while they waited for permission to leave the aeroplane.

After years of not seeing each other, Marjorie and Edna Parkinton had found themselves thrown together in Amsterdam at the start of a river cruise holiday the previous year. The two women had ended up sharing a room following a mix-up with Edna's booking.

This holiday in the Scottish Highlands was to be their third joint trip since fate brought them together. Marjorie couldn't help feeling she had somehow slumbered into the friendship – or companionship – from her side, if truth be told. Almost in spite of herself, Marjorie was growing to like Edna, although acknowledging most of her cousin-in-law's vulgarities and behaviours would never change. But whether they could ever be truly close depended on

Marjorie's ability to forgive, if not forget, the battering Edna had inflicted on the love of her life whom she would miss every day until she too left this earth.

The captain's announcement and the 'unfasten your seatbelt' sign signalled it was time to leave.

"Come on, Marge, it's time for our jollies." Edna's holler broke through her musings.

Marjorie exhaled, realising she had been holding her breath. "Good," she said.

"Do you need me to call the stewardess to assist you?"

Marjorie glared into Edna's deep brown eyes.

"No, thank you. I'm quite capable of disembarking an aircraft on my own, as you well know. If you would be kind enough to reach for my hand luggage from the overhead locker, though, I'd appreciate it." Marjorie's small stature was a hindrance at times, especially when she had to depend on Edna, who was bound to gloat.

The predictable grin as Edna stood in the narrow aisle told her she was right. Her cousin-in-law's bulk blocked the way of a hen party trying to exit. There followed a slow and deliberate removal of their hand luggage while she commandeered the aisle. It was intentional, of that there was no doubt. Edna held her position, waiting for Marjorie to get up from her seat while the complaining crowd, who had been raucous throughout the flight, murmured amongst themselves. A few of them were tutting loudly.

"Hurry up Mrs. We ain't got all day." One girl further down the line yelled.

Edna rounded on them before barking. "On the contrary; your party doesn't start until eight at Glenmoriston Townhouse, was it? Before that, though, you're gonna try to meet up with a few Inverness laddies. After all, it's Carla's last night of freedom. By my reckoning, you've got plenty of time."

The young woman immediately behind Edna flushed red from the neck up. "Sorry if we got on your nerves; we didn't mean to be so loud."

"It's quite all right," Marjorie broke the impasse. "We were young once. Now come along, Edna. I might need your help to disembark after all."

Once they were off the aeroplane, Marjorie was pleased there was no further fracas between Edna and the hen party, just a little muttering about the 'old bag' giving them a hard time.

Edna smirked. "That told 'em. They didn't need to tell the whole bloomin' plane what they were up to. Next time they'll be better behaved."

"I doubt that, and for my part, I enjoyed their excitement. It's rare one hears unbridled joy these days." *Far better than listening to you crowing on about your days as a singer,* went unsaid.

"I can't see what's pleasant about suffering a bunch of silly young women giggling the whole way up here. But, if you say so, Marge."

"And I can't see why you feel the need to get into an argument with complete strangers over trivial things. It really is beyond me."

Edna thrust Marjorie's hand luggage at her. "Let's get a move on. I'm looking forward to seeing Horace again and I bet you can't wait to see your Fred."

"His name is Frederick." Marjorie gritted her teeth. *And mine is Marjorie*, she thought, but said, "What I am looking forward to is seeing more of the Highlands. Ralph loved Scotland, but spent most of his time up here fishing, so I often passed on his trips and let him go with…" Marjorie paused; she'd almost let slip he went with Johnson the chauffeur, a sure way of reminding Edna of her perceived misfortunes.

"I have to admit the extra few days at Loch Ness could be exciting, as long as we don't go out at night." Edna blew out a breath, wiping her brow.

"That's an odd thing to say."

"What?"

"Never mind." Marjorie was also looking forward to the extended stay. The itinerary had been altered the week before they were due to travel because regulatory authorities ordered compulsory renovation work at their onward hotel. Faith Weathers, their tour guide, had arranged for them to stay by the loch for four nights rather than two. The hotel apparently overlooked the great loch, which she had longed to visit for many years. Had she gone with Ralph, he would have brought rods and tackle and left her to her own devices. She felt a pang of guilt as that thought crossed her mind. Nevertheless, the change in itinerary had been ideal from her perspective.

"Where is everybody?" Edna glanced around.

"By everybody, I assume you mean Horace? Faith's over there." Marjorie observed their regular tour guide standing on ceremony with a large sign reading: Queen River and Land Tours, Highland Tour.

"Is that Daisy with her?"

"So it is," said Marjorie, happy to see the youthful woman. Daisy had been on the Amsterdam tour. Younger than Faith, she was vivacious, accommodating and genial.

"Don't worry about your luggage, Lady Marjorie," Faith called. "The cases are being collected and put on the bus for you."

Edna huffed. "What about mine?"

"And yours, Edna." Faith gave them a warm smile as they approached while ticking them off on a list. Young Daisy's grin widened, showing Marjorie she remembered Edna well. *Once met, never forgotten.*

Faith shook their hands. "We'll be leaving for the coach station in half an hour to pick up the rest of the party. Some have decided to travel up by coach. Before going on to Loch Ness, we'll stop at a popular tourist destination called Rogie Falls. We've had to split the party between two hotels... I forgot to ask, how was your flight?"

"Noisy," said Edna, shooting Marjorie a glare.

Faith's eyebrows raised, "Oh?"

"Our flight was fine," said Marjorie.

Edna cackled. "If you enjoy listening to silly young women droning on about the opposite sex."

Daisy couldn't hide a grin.

Faith gave a nod, eyes brightening. "I almost forgot to tell you... Horace Tyler arrived about fifteen minutes ago and went to the coffee shop. He said if I saw you, to let you know where he was in case you wanted to join him."

"Trust Horace to make himself comfortable. You coming, Marge?"

Marjorie had long since given up hope Edna would tire of using the diminutive of her name. Nothing worked; if she didn't react, it continued, and if she refused to reply, it still made no difference. Edna would not change and even though it grated rather than annoyed her these days, she didn't believe her cousin-in-law could help herself. Diminutives is what she did; they weren't reserved for Marjorie, so why fight it? "I'll be along in a moment. You go ahead."

Edna scampered along the concourse, repositioning her red wig, which she had insisted suited Scotland best when she had put it on before leaving this morning. Marjorie swallowed the lump in her throat before addressing Faith.

"I forgot to ask before taking you up on Major Jeffries's generous offer. Will Edna and I be in separate rooms?"

"In the original booking, there would have been a couple sharing, but I changed it and nabbed you an extra room. The owner of Nessie's Lochside Hotel, where our half of the tour party is staying, was very accommodating, particularly after I extended our stay. The hotel's newly opened, so she was only too pleased to help."

Marjorie felt the tension in her neck release. "That's wonderful."

"We had more difficulty extending our booking for the extra nights at the second hotel. It's hugely popular with tourists, but for the added days, they've squeezed some of our guests into their self-catering lodges while offering to provide meals at the hotel, but none of that applies to you. Daisy will stay with that half of the party and we're combining for organised tours. From the few conversations I've had with Nessa, she sounds like a bundle of energy. I think we're going to enjoy our stay."

"Nessie's Lochside Hotel, you said? Isn't that the nickname of the Loch Ness Monster?"

Faith tittered. "Yes. Nessa owns the hotel and ended up naming it after the infamous monster. Both our hotels are close to Loch Ness's shore, and hers is the fulfilment of a childhood dream. I'm sure we'll find out more about the area when we meet her."

A few other guests arrived to check in with the two guides and ask for instructions. Marjorie saw a dour-looking lanky man who she heard snapping at Daisy. Faith intervened, and they both returned to welcoming guests and marking names off their respective clipboard lists. Somehow, seeing Faith and the clipboard gave an air of security and familiarity. A perfect choice for her line of work, Faith was efficient and affable, a woman who could speak to anyone with ease. Even Marjorie, with all her dinner party hostess experience, admired her for that. There was no sign of Frederick, whom she had been looking out for even though he wasn't *hers,* as Edna annoyingly teased. She hoped he hadn't changed his mind about joining them. He and Horace were pleasant distractions and helped keep Edna from irritating her too much.

Marjorie headed inside the coffee bar.

Horace stood to shake her hand. "Good to see you again, Marjorie. I hope you don't mind. I ordered you a pot of tea. The service is slow, and I didn't want you to miss out."

"It's lovely to see you too," she said. "And I don't mind at all." Marjorie stared disapprovingly at the mug. She preferred drinking tea from a cup, but it was a nice thought and she mustn't be churlish. She and Edna had met

Horace on the Amsterdam tour, whereas Frederick they only met recently during a Romanian holiday and river cruise. A grateful guest had gifted them this holiday after they solved a murder proving his innocence.

"Fred's getting the coach up from Glasgow. He's been visiting his son down there. The Gang of Four will be back together very soon." Horace winked, and Edna snorted.

"I don't want to be in a gang. Besides, I count Faith as one of us, so perhaps we should be an adult version of Enid Blyton's *Famous Five*."

Edna chortled. "Good one, Marge. She does have a sense of humour when she's not being such a snob."

"So do you when you're not being a slob," retorted Marjorie.

Horace laughed loudly and he and Edna emitted joint snorts. "I wouldn't mind being part of your gang, Lady Marjorie, but *Famous Five* will do, on condition there are no murders."

"That, I'm afraid I cannot guarantee, especially staying beside the misty shores of Loch Ness," she chuckled but inwardly scolded herself as Edna turned pale. *Best not to make light of such things in view of our history.*

Chapter 2

Whilst Edna and Horace chatted, Marjorie sipped tea, whiling away the time people-watching. She was observing other guests joining their tour party meeting with Faith and Daisy. The lanky man she had witnessed snapping at Daisy was wearing the floor out, pacing back and forth. Every so often he surreptitiously did what she herself was doing, checking who was checking in, but he appeared to be looking out for someone. Perhaps someone was joining him. Marjorie hoped he was staying at the second hotel Faith had mentioned. His scowl was hardly fit for a relaxing holiday.

With people blocking her way so she couldn't see him any longer, Marjorie surveyed others coming and going who were closer to the window. A couple of police officers came inside and sat at a table having a whispered conversation. The man removed his hat, revealing curly blond locks and a patch of dry skin at his hairline. He only appeared to be half-listening to the female officer whose back was towards her. Marjorie wondered whether he, too, was looking out for someone or was just not interested in his colleague's conversation.

"Marge?"

"I'm sorry, were you speaking to me?" Marjorie looked at Edna.

Edna rolled her eyes. "It's time to go. Faith's been waving at us for ages."

Marjorie felt it ill advised to argue the fact they hadn't been inside the café for that long, so she let the exaggeration go. Once they stepped out of the terminal building, Marjorie drew in a deep, cleansing breath of cool but invigorating Scottish autumnal air, savouring its freshness.

The gathered tour party thus far comprised people arriving via three separate flights. Horace had already told them he'd flown in from Gatwick, Marjorie and Edna had arrived from Manchester and the rest had come via Heathrow Airport. Faith explained that passengers and their baggage on the Heathrow flight had to be transferred to another aircraft because of a mechanical failure of the first aeroplane. Faith and Daisy assembled all the expected tour guests together, including a few stragglers, one of which was the tall man Marjorie had noticed inside the terminal.

After boarding the luxury coach, Marjorie, Edna and Horace found comfortable seats midway along. Edna was happy for Marjorie to take the window seat because it meant she could chat with Horace, who sat by himself.

"I'll save a seat for Fred," he said, putting a bag on the window seat next to him. The coach was only half full, so it didn't really matter.

"Frederick," Marjorie muttered under her breath, but there was no use arguing the point. Horace and Edna were so alike they could have been related. Correcting them would be like trying to deter a couple of teenage friends from misbehaving in class. Still, she was grateful Horace and Edna got on so well because it meant her cousin-in-law would be preoccupied enough not to annoy her too much.

They were finally on the way to the coach station. Horace and Edna resumed their chattering while Marjorie stared out of the window.

She rolled her eyes when once more disturbed by Edna cackling and Horace snorting. Sometimes Marjorie felt ashamed of her behaviour towards Edna, but each time she thought she could rise above it, the other woman did, or said, something to rile her. Whether by design or accident, Marjorie hadn't yet been able to fathom. Their upbringings had been worlds apart, but that wasn't the issue. Marjorie had never looked down on people because of class or upbringing. Besides the hindrances from the past, she just wasn't comfortable with Edna's loud and brash 'speak-before-you-think' ways. They often resulted in altercations like the one with the young women on the aeroplane. It occasionally appeared as though her cousin-in-law was purposely spoiling for a fight. Marjorie couldn't help but wonder if Edna was still harbouring a grudge about her mother's struggles, which she blamed on Ralph's grandfather, father and, in turn, Ralph for inheriting the family fortune. On the other hand, Edna could still be grieving the loss of her husband. Marjorie could understand and empathise with the latter. After Ralph had died and the intense sadness that decorum hadn't allowed her to display diminished, she would feel suddenly angry for no reason. If it hadn't been for decades of coaching to keep her emotions under control, something being born into the aristocracy dictated, she could have easily lashed out.

As the wife of another aristocrat and a respected businessman, duty had always come before feelings, but no-one should be in any doubt that beneath the exterior there had been a broken, but still beating, heart. If Marjorie hadn't met her young friend, Rachel Prince, now Jacobi-Prince, these past few years would have been unbearable. Rachel had no idea how therapeutic her friendship had been and was now the closest thing she had to a granddaughter, holding a special place in her heart. Rachel also understood duty. Not just through her Christian faith and her work as a police officer, but she had learned it from her parents; her father was a village vicar and her mother a vicar's wife who had performed a role that Marjorie herself had so often, albeit under different circumstances, undertaken. Perhaps, as well as the hurt she had been mulling over for the past few days, Marjorie's reactions to Edna were also in some way linked to elements of grief that she could never show.

The coach drew to a halt, bringing Marjorie's reminiscences to a standstill. "Thank heavens," she said. Then, as if to prove herself the eternal nemesis, Edna nudged her.

"What's up, Marge? You thinking about your Fred?"

"He's not *my* Fred." She didn't bother adding again that the man's name was Frederick. "And do keep your voice down."

"Whatever you say, Marge."

"Here's the man of the moment now," said Horace.

With Marjorie being short and the headrests high, she didn't see Frederick until he was almost upon them. He was sensibly wearing a trilby hat, protecting his bald head from the elements, and he looked just as smart as he had just six weeks ago when they had first met in Romania. *He really should do something about his choice of shirt, though.* That was her only criticism. Frederick wore checked shirts under suit jackets which rarely matched, especially when he wore a striped tie like the one he had on today which clashed.

"Hello again," his grey eyes crinkled into a shy smile when they met Marjorie's, and she felt a slight flutter of her heart.

Quickly telling herself to get a grip and regain control, she nodded a greeting. "Hello. I hope you had a pleasant journey."

"It was beautiful, actually. The scenery on the way up here was exquisite." The sun caught his eyes, causing them to dance as they creased once more into a smile.

"Our flight was all right. Thanks for asking," Edna interrupted, hating to be left out of any conversation. "Apart from a rowdy hen party, that is."

"Give the man a chance, Edna," said Horace, standing to shake Frederick's hand once other passengers had passed. "Here, I've saved a seat for you. I take it you don't mind the window? Edna and I are having a bit of a catch-up."

Marjorie had to stop herself suggesting they swap seating companions altogether, but it would appear too forward, and she didn't want to give Frederick the wrong impression. More importantly, it wouldn't do to give Edna any more ammunition to hurl her way.

"I don't mind at all. Thanks for thinking of me. Faith looks well, doesn't she? More relaxed than the last time we were with her."

Horace moved further into the aisle to allow Frederick room to slide into a seat next to the window. "She had a lot on her mind last time out, didn't she?" He winked. "Besides, she's got young Daisy to help on this tour. We met Daisy on the Amsterdam holiday when we became friends. A nice young thing, good looking, too."

"And far too young for you, Horace Tyler," scolded Edna.

"You can't blame a man for wishing he was a tad younger," Horace smirked.

"A tad! You're quite a few decades out there, mate." Edna giggled and Horace snorted.

Marjorie hoped their next destination would be enough to make this journey worthwhile.

Chapter 3

After travelling for around thirty minutes, the coach pulled in at the carpark for Rogie Falls, parking side-on close to the exit. Other than their coach, there were just a few cars and a motorhome, which was as well. Marjorie felt the driver would not have been able to manoeuvre the large vehicle to park in the way he had otherwise. Faith spoke through a microphone from the front of the coach. Marjorie couldn't see her from the window seat, but she could hear.

"We've arrived at the carpark for Rogie Falls."

"Talk about stating the bloomin' obvious," said Edna.

Marjorie smiled. 'Stating the bloomin' obvious' was one of her cousin-in-law's favourite expressions.

Faith continued. "I'll be taking The Salmon Trail, which is the shortest route to the falls, at about half a mile long. For those of you would like to join me, the trail comprises a fairly even gravel path right up to the falls where there is a viewpoint. There's a steepish slope down, so if any of you would prefer to wander around the woodland trails closer to the carpark you're welcome to do so. For those who prefer a more challenging walk and aren't averse to uneven and muddy terrain, please follow Daisy, who will take The Riverside Trail. It's only about three quarters of a mile, but you'll need to be relatively fit and wearing sturdy shoes. There are toilets in the carpark here if you would like to use them instead of the one on the coach which is best saved for when we're travelling. Both groups will set off in around ten minutes to give you time to use the facilities if you need to, and to stretch your legs. Whatever you decide to do, we'll meet back at the carpark in two hours. You're welcome to leave heavier bags onboard, or stay on the coach if you wish, as the driver will remain here for the duration."

"I've heard Rogie Falls are spectacular at this time of year, so I'm keen to take a stroll. It'll be even more enjoyable with the forest leaves changing colour," said Horace.

"You mean to say you haven't been here before," Marjorie said, teasing. Horace had a tendency to show off, but for good reason, she had to admit. He was well travelled and had been to many places for business and pleasure that made her world travels pale in comparison. They had discovered on the previous holiday that his mother was Romanian, but he had been reluctant to share any more of that history. No doubt Edna would prise it out of him one day. Horace Tyler owned an avionics firm and still seemed involved in its running, despite being seventy-eight. Some men, it appeared, were reluctant to relinquish control. Having said that, so were some women. Marjorie monitored the business Ralph had built up and in which she held controlling shares.

"I hate to admit it," Horace replied, "but I've only ever visited factories and airports in Scotland, which is why I'm really looking forward to being a tourist."

"I thought I might stay behind, but if you think it's worth the effort, I vote for the shorter route," said Edna, sounding hesitant.

Marjorie worried about Edna sometimes. She had noticed, since becoming reacquainted on the first holiday, that the larger woman became breathless after a few hundred yards and, although weight was a factor, Marjorie felt it was more to do with the cancer her cousin-in-law had suffered, or a hangover from its treatment. She admired Edna's determination to live life to the full, and for not playing the pity card, considering it had clearly left her less agile than before. Also, the treatment had given her chronic alopecia, hence the ownership of a multitude of wigs.

"I'm happy to take the shorter route," Marjorie said with empathy.

Any sympathy soon evaporated when Edna replied. "I'm not sure two hours will be long enough for you to make it there and back anyway, Marge. Are you sure you'll manage?"

Horace intervened before Marjorie was tempted to say something she might regret. "Come on then. Let's join the throng. Are you coming, Fred?"

Frederick rolled his eyes. He loathed being called Fred as much as she disliked being called Marge, but he would have to accept that Horace and Edna would continue to shorten his name, or be driven mad by it.

Once they were off the coach, they joined a group of fifteen people gathered around Faith. Daisy and a smaller party, Faith told them, had already set off. Following a head count, Faith led their assembly along a wide path through a pleasant forest lined with evergreen and deciduous trees.

"When we get to the falls, keep an eye out for salmon. I'm told this is the best time of year to catch sight of them leaping."

Marjorie could just about hear Faith above the merry chatter of tourists.

Edna nudged her, "Hurry up, Marge... Use your stick."

Marjorie rarely used her walking stick, but was sorely tempted to use it on her cousin-in-law. On this occasion, she inwardly conceded that on the current terrain, it might be necessary. Reluctantly, she removed the fold-up crutch from her large handbag.

Edna smirked but, for once, had the good sense to say nothing.

Horace picked up a long branch of wood from the ground and strolled on ahead, using it as a support, making Marjorie feel much better.

"Come along Edna. Keep up," he called back.

Marjorie was happy when her companion hurried ahead to join him. Edna's breathing might not be so good on the upward slopes, but she was keeping pace with the group on the downward path, although Faith was setting a steady pace for the mixed-age flock.

Frederick was chatting to the miserable, skinny, middle-aged man Marjorie had noticed at the airport. The latter was dressed for the countryside, and the weather, wearing a deerstalker, hiking boots and a navy-blue puffer jacket. He towered over the shorter Frederick. Marjorie herself was wearing comfortable, flat shoes and her favourite dark brown winter coat over a woollen jumper and tweed skirt. She wore the tweed on the insistence of her housekeeper, Mrs Ratton, who explained it would go down a storm in the Highlands. She had to admit it didn't look out of place and was warm.

It was turning out to be a crisp but cool autumnal day, with a bright low sun sending dancing speckles of light through the trees that caught the path. The light cast gentle swaying branch shadows onto the ground they were walking on. Marjorie inhaled through her nose, appreciating the fragrant wafts of pine as she took her time to enjoy the ramble.

A young couple just ahead only had eyes for each other. They giggled and chattered, holding hands, clearly oblivious to anything or anyone else.

Young love, she thought. *It's all part of the cycle of life. I wonder if theirs will be a lasting relationship or one of many on the road to discovering a soulmate.* Her mind was about to retreat to her younger days when she and Ralph first began their courtship, but something prevented it from doing so. A sharp, though not unkind, rebuke came from a rounded man in his late forties. The man removed a cap revealing thinning, black hair.

"You might want to take in some of the scenery, you two." A wonderful baritone Scottish accent was unmistakeable. The man waved his arms in a general direction before thrusting his hands inside a heavy black overcoat.

The teenage girl pouted, "We are, Dad, but there's nothing to see here except for trees. I've seen it all before."

No sooner had she complained than the roar of a waterfall reached their ears as they rounded a bend, drawing closer to the falls. The rumbling sound arrested their attention. Soon afterwards, they arrived at a spot where the rest of the group had already come to a halt beside a suspension bridge. The short bridge crossed over a height and afforded a closer view of the spectacular waterfall. Spray from the falls reached Marjorie's nostrils.

Marjorie almost fell to the ground as someone barged her from behind.

Chapter 4

Marjorie felt lightheaded as she clenched both hands around the head of her stick. She saw her assailant disappear into the crowd.

Frederick appeared by her side, taking her arm.

"Are you all right, Marjorie? You look pale."

"I'm fine. I must have let go of my stick for a moment."

"Come over here. There are salmon." Frederick guided her away from the crowd.

Marjorie wouldn't normally be enthusiastic about fish; that was her husband's forte, but to see salmon leap! Now that was something else. Frederick led her away from the crowd, some of whom were already crossing the bridge in small groups.

"Thank you. I don't think I'd be able to stretch to swaying my way across that anyway," she said. Especially now, she thought. Her heart still beat rapidly, wondering whether the nudge was deliberate, but common sense told her it was almost certainly clumsiness rather than anything else.

"The bridge is safe enough as long as they don't overcrowd it. Look! Over there, at the edge of the falls."

Sure enough, Marjorie watched, as first one, then another salmon attempted the giant leap against the heavy downward water and gravity. "Poor things. Surely they won't make it?"

"They will, or they'll die trying," said Frederick. "They've got a little help, though. There's a manmade salmon ladder just there. It's important to lend a helping hand sometimes and encourage breeding, otherwise they'll be overfished. I expect we'll be eating a fair bit of salmon over the next few days."

Marjorie had been about to ask him where his salmon knowledge came from, but baulked instead at the reminder of where the food she ate came from. "I realise it's hypocritical, but I prefer to disassociate myself from the natural world and what ends up on my plate."

Frederick laughed, eyes shining again. "You're not alone in that. Jock and I were having a similar conversation on the way down here."

"Who's Jock?" Marjorie didn't want to let on she had noticed the man Frederick had been speaking to. The man who had almost knocked her down moments ago.

"A surly fellow I just met; he's interesting to talk to but a bit nippy, as the Scots would say."

"Nippy meaning annoying?"

"More nippy, meaning sharp-tongued. There he is, over there." Frederick pointed to the man in the deerstalker.

Marjorie scrutinised the ignorant man, this time face-on. The man named Jock had a sandy brown unruly beard and moustache; the colour matching a fringe protruding from his hat. He was even taller close-up, lanky as she had already surmised and appeared to be arguing with a couple of a similar age to himself. It was perhaps as well he wasn't more bulky or he could have done her serious damage. "I see what you mean about being surly – or nippy. Is he travelling with those people?" Were they who he had appeared to be looking out for at the airport she wondered?

"I don't think so. He told me he was on his own. The reason I found him interesting was he said he grew up in a village somewhere around these parts, a place called Scraghead, closer to Loch Ness than here." Frederick lowered his voice. "He's writing, what he calls, an Exposé of life around the loch."

Marjorie raised an eyebrow.

"How much of that was marketing talk and how much was true, I couldn't say," Frederick continued.

"So basically, he's writing a memoir or an autobiography," said Marjorie.

"I guess so, but one that uncovers some dirty linen, according to him, anyhow," added Frederick.

"Well, let's hope he doesn't name names or he might end up in court for slander. As you say, it's most likely a marketing spiel. Unless, of course, he's met the Loch Ness Monster in person. Now that would be worth reading about." Marjorie chuckled. "Seriously, though, I would imagine an ordinary person writing a memoir for public consumption would need to sensationalise it. Unless it's about a career, or something that interests people. It must be hard to coax people to buy memoirs otherwise. I'm assuming he's not famous, but of course, he might be. Did he say he'd written anything else?"

"I didn't get the chance to ask him. We arrived at the falls and he skulked off while I was listening to Faith giving instructions and warnings about taking care on the suspension bridge."

Before barging into me, thought Marjorie.

"Not to mention Horace and Edna turning up."

"My condolences," Marjorie laughed.

"What you staring at, Marge?"

Marjorie jumped, wondering whether Edna had heard their conversation, but there was no indication she had.

"Salmon." Marjorie turned her attention away from the man called Jock and back to the marvellous fish battling the elements.

"Ain't we lucky. Mick said it's unusual to see them at this time of day, but he reckons it's because of the recent rainfall."

"Who's Mick?" asked Frederick.

"The big guy over there. The one with the love-struck teenagers. He's a widower, says he used to come here twice a year for a holiday. Apparently his wife loved the area, especially Loch Ness. He also told us we have to be careful of the mists over the loch." Edna shuddered. "They can come down real quick and it's easy to lose your footing. You'd better get used to using that stick of yours, Marge."

Marjorie watched the man who had rebuked the teenagers, trying again to encourage them to take their eyes off each other. Poor man. She turned back to Edna and saw Horace approaching. "You're hardly stealth-like yourself, dear, but I'm looking forward to walking through the mists, especially if we get a peek at Nessie."

Edna frowned. "You shouldn't joke about such things. No use tempting fate."

Marjorie felt her eyes widen.

"Edna believes the monster is real." Horace lowered his voice. "She's worried about our prolonged stay by the loch."

"You never said! In fact, you told me quite the opposite this morning," said Marjorie.

"Bravado. I thought you'd laugh at me if I told you, and I didn't realise we'd be staying so close to it."

Astounded, Marjorie wondered if her cousin-in-law ever read any of the literature sent prior to the tour.

"Anyway," Edna continued, folding her arms. "There's no need to whisper. Mick agrees with me, as do countless others on the internet." Edna glowered at Horace, who was struggling not to laugh.

"Well, if it's on the internet, it must be true," teased Frederick.

"You'd better watch out. That bald head of yours will stand out like a big fish, so I'd stay away from the water if I were you," Edna countered.

Marjorie was about to rebuke her cousin-in-law for being so rude, but Frederick laughed as he pulled his hat further down his head. "I'll take it under advisement."

After spending a pleasant thirty minutes gazing at the waterfall and watching more than a few salmon make it to the top, it was time to leave. Faith called the party back together to start the return journey.

Edna introduced Marjorie and Frederick to Mick before setting off with Horace. Marjorie found herself at the back of the group again on the upward slope. She was pleased the two men were deep in conversation, not noticing her slowing down as a spasm engulfed her, leaving her struggling to breathe.

A bout of pneumonia earlier in the year had left her with occasional breathless attacks, which always took her by surprise. Her slow recovery had prevented her from attending Rachel's wedding in the summer and had been a major blow, but she had followed her doctor's advice. Marjorie had persuaded her chauffeur, Johnson, to drive her down to Southampton to wave the happy couple off on their honeymoon cruise and surprise her friend with a cabin upgrade as a wedding gift.

She had forgotten the attacks could be triggered by the cold. Each time she thought she'd seen the back of them, another would come, arriving like a bolt out of nowhere, but they usually passed quickly. Edna was ignorant of the pneumonia episode. In fact, most people were apart from those closest to her. There had been no issues during the trip to Romania, despite the pollution in Cluj Napoca. The Scottish air would aid her recuperation. Of this, she was certain. Stopping for a few moments to calm herself, she took a few slow, deep breaths, just like the physiotherapist who had seen her at home had taught her to. She knew this would slow her heart rate down and help her recover from the spasm. Marjorie had almost made it to the top of the incline when the attack came on and felt well enough to continue the brief journey remaining.

As the crowd ahead got further away, Marjorie had an uncomfortable sensation she wasn't alone.

Chapter 5

As the stragglers, including Frederick and the man called Mick, vanished into the distance, the sun disappeared behind a cloud and a freezing chill filled the air, piercing Marjorie's bones. She had arrived on the flat and tried to pick up speed, but when she did so, pain coursed through her lower right rib cage, hitting the spot where the pneumonia had struck. Forced to stop again to give herself a rest, Marjorie's heart quickened when she heard twigs cracking and footsteps approaching from the trees on her right. The pounding in her chest made it more difficult to control her breathing, which sounded raspy.

"Are you all right?"

Marjorie looked up as the sour Jock emerged from the shadows, speaking in a surprisingly deep, though gruff, voice. The sight of the man who had almost knocked her over made her feet feel like lead.

He came closer, but not on top of her. She found her voice. "Quite. Thank you. I didn't realise anyone else was around."

"I was just taking a wee stroll through the forest. I like to be alone to contemplate things, and a noisy crowd ruins a pleasant walk."

Brood more like, thought Marjorie, checking his sharp, thin features behind the hair growth, but she said, "I know what you mean. I've heard the same said about golf."

The shifty look in the man's light brown eyes made her feel uncomfortable. Thick lips pouted, and she noticed he was holding something in his left hand. He dropped a rock to the ground when he saw her looking.

"You can ne'er be too careful when roaming alone. Yer shouldn't get isolated in these parts. It's dangerous."

Mouth dry, she wasn't sure if she detected a threat, or a sensible warning?

"You're Lady Marjorie, aren't yer?"

"I am, but you have the advantage over me. I don't know who you are." Marjorie wasn't sure why she didn't admit to knowing who he was, but it was too late to retract. She tried to control her breathing before dizziness overwhelmed her.

The man held out a scrawny hand with long, thin fingers. "The name's Jock McGuire. I was having a wee chat with your friend Fred Mackworth. I'm surprised he didnae mention me."

There was an arrogance and a challenge in the statement. Jock McGuire's scrutinising gaze made her feel even more uncomfortable, but she wouldn't let her bodily reactions overwhelm her. She stood as tall as she could and held the man's intent look.

"Frederick…" Why must everyone resort to diminutives? "…mentioned meeting an author. I don't recall him giving a name. Is that you?"

Jock's lips upturned but didn't quite make a smile. "Aye, it is indeed."

After shaking hands and establishing a truce, they started moving, Marjorie willing her legs not to give up on her. Jock kept his pace slow and steady alongside hers. An uncomfortable silence developed, which Marjorie broke. "Frederick mentioned the author – you – came from the Loch Ness area. It must have been very special growing up surrounded by such natural beauty. I expect you know these parts well."

"Well enough. But don't yer be taken in by the scenery. There's wickedness aroond every corner. Don't ye forget that, Lady Marjorie."

Paranoid as well as surly, Marjorie thought. She wondered what Frederick had found interesting when speaking to this aggressive man. "We can dispense with the formalities. Call me Marjorie, please…" she hesitated, "This evil you're speaking of. Is that what you're writing about? Frederick said you were writing a memoir."

"Did he now?"

The pointed chin sharpened, and Marjorie noticed a pulsating temple. She had struck a nerve.

"It's nae a memoir, more of a revelation. At least it will be once it's oot."

"I'm intrigued. What exactly will you be revealing? I hope it will not spoil my perception of the wonderful Highlands." She gave a nervous laugh. Something in his eyes staring straight ahead with a flintlike determination made her wish she hadn't lost sight of the others.

"Things people aroond here, and some as don't live here no more, willnae want to see in print, that's for sure. Look. Let's not mess aboot. Yer friend, *Frederick,* told me you're a bit of an amateur sleuth, and that you've solved a few murders in yer time. Ye should warn him not to go shooting his mouth off about stuff like that. People in these parts – especially where we're going – donae like others delving into their pasts. I thought I should warn yer, that's all."

"Frederick exaggerates. I'm no sleuth, and I can assure you, Mr McGuire, my only interest lies in the exquisite scenery and the famous loch."

Jock shook his head. "Have it your way, but I still think ye should watch yer back. Yer friend might already have landed you in danger."

With the dry throat and rib pain returning, Marjorie found herself unable to speak, but pushed on. Was there a veiled threat beneath this apparent friendly warning or was he really so paranoid that he imagined villains hid behind every tree, and why did he barge into her earlier? The rock carrying through the forest suggested paranoia. Her confidence returned, and the pain disappeared when, with deep relief, she saw Horace and Frederick heading in their direction. Emboldened, she said, "I would have thought, if there is anything to fear, as the exposer of secrets, Mr McGuire, it might be you who needs to heed your own warning."

McGuire rounded on her, blocking her path; he stopped walking. She found his eyes boring down into hers. Only this time they weren't threatening, instead they were filled with fear. "You're right aboot that. It wouldn't surprise me if someone tried to kill me. If they succeed, ye might get to put yer sleuthing skills to the test. If I were you, though, I'd still tell yer mate to keep his gob shut."

Marjorie was happy when Jock McGuire stomped off in the carpark's direction, giving Frederick a nod as he passed the approaching duo. Horace reached her first. "Edna was worried about you, so Fred and I thought we'd better come and find you. What did that man say to you just now? You look pale."

"Nothing of any importance. I got a chill when the sun went in, which slowed me down. Mr McGuire accompanied me to make sure I was all right." *And then another chill from the conversation I've just had*, she mused, but didn't want to put a dampener on the holiday because of an overimaginative mind. Perhaps this cloak-and-dagger stuff was all part of Jock McGuire's marketing ploy. He had her hooked. Whilst she believed it would be full of stuff and nonsense, she would definitely buy his book.

Being the gentleman he was, Horace removed his scarf and wrapped it around her neck. Both men held their arms out, and she packed her stick away.

"Allow us to escort you back to the warmth," Horace said.

The sun reappeared almost as soon as he finished the sentence, dispelling any darkness Jock McGuire had left hovering over her. Marjorie laughed out loud, more from relief than humour.

"Did he tell you anything about what's in that book he's writing?" Frederick asked, clearly enthralled by Jock.

"He mentioned it, but gave no details, I'm afraid. However, he said you told him I was a sleuth who had solved murders in the past. He seemed quite fixated on the idea, and appears to have a vivid imagination. Perhaps it's best if you don't mention it to anyone else. Remember, some people don't get out into the world that much, and Loch Ness has enough fables and myths of its own without adding murder to the equation."

Frederick took the rebuke in good spirit. "You might be right. I've had a few weird conversations already today."

"And now I feel I must warn you that Edna's determined to convince us all the Loch Ness Monster's real. It must be something in the water," Horace remarked before snorting loudly just as they arrived back at the coach.

Chapter 6

From the road, Nessie's Lochside Hotel looked more like an enormous house than a hotel, sympathetically built to fit in with its surroundings. It was nestled in the hills about half a mile from the shores of Loch Ness. They turned right at a large black sign with the hotel's name standing out in white, entering through wide metal gates. The driver navigated the coach up a winding, narrow lane before stopping in front of the hotel. Marjorie counted fifteen passengers, plus Faith, disembarking.

A sprightly woman aged around fifty, with permed black hair, rushed out to greet them before their luggage was even removed. Two men, one of whom looked to be in his mid-seventies and the other in his twenties, accompanied her and set about sorting through cases with the driver.

The tiny, exuberant woman had a high-pitched, lilting voice. "Welcome to Nessie's. We're delighted to have you here. I'm Vanessa, but my friends call me Nessa. I named the hotel after the mythical monster, and I like to think it's also named partly after myself. I feel it adds a charm to the place, as well as ensuring potential guests know where it is. You'll find all our rooms comfortable with central heating, which you can control through your own remote thermostatic handset... there are ensuites with showers in most, and a few of the rooms have baths. You're only our second large company of guests because the hotel only opened three weeks ago, but don't you worry, I've been in the hospitality business all my life and we've acquired the best staff to look after you, with a brilliant chef from Edinburgh. There are other guests staying as well. If you have any questions at all, just ask. You're going to have the best four nights ever, and I hope you'll come again and again and tell your friends about us..."

Nessa barely stopped for breath and continued to regale the new arrivals with information about the hotel, shaking each person's hand vigorously, until her eyes widened and she came to a sudden stop, along with her chatter.

Jock McGuire stared down at the diminutive woman who was no taller than Marjorie. Jock gave a tight-lipped half-smile, but the stare was hard.

"Hello Nessa."

"Phil McGuire?" The proprietor's voice could only just be heard and was suddenly shaky. "I'm sorry, I don't have you down on my list and we're fully booked." Nessa recovered enough to put on an air of indifference, though sounding slightly smug about there being no room for her surprise guest. She dropped her eyes away from his and Marjorie watched as the older man, who had been dealing with their luggage, appeared by her side, glaring at Jock McGuire.

Faith also froze. She had been about to introduce herself, but was astute enough to sense the bad vibe and appeared concerned. She said nothing.

"I go by the name of Jock these days." He looked down at the woman holding an open foolscap in trembling hands. "There, I think you'll find that name on your guest list. Jock McGuire."

Nessa's lips narrowed as it forced her to acknowledge the man again, staring upwards. He was a good sixteen inches taller than she was. "You're welcome to stay at my hotel as long as you've left trouble behind you."

Jock grinned maliciously. "Can't be making any promises." He shrugged. "I'm here to work. You might be interested to know I'm writing a book about these parts." He brushed past her, leaving the startled Nessa staring after him, bewitched. Jock, AKA Phil, strolled nonchalantly into the hotel. The older man whispered something in Nessa's ear, and marched inside the hotel after the unwelcome guest.

Nessa's hand still trembled as she took Faith's proffered hand, once she came out of her unpleasant trance.

"I'm so pleased to meet you at last. I'm Faith Weathers, we spoke on the phone…"

With most people's attention focussed on their luggage and some already climbing the steps into the hotel, only a few people had noticed the awkward interaction between Nessa and Jock McGuire.

"Judging by that encounter. I doubt he's left trouble behind. Quite the opposite, I'd say," said Edna.

"I'm inclined to agree with you," said Marjorie. "Whatever he's here for… it isn't pleasant. But I think we already knew that."

"There's history between those two. Mark my words," said Horace.

Edna raised a tinted eyebrow. "Seriously, Horace. You've got to be the king of stating the bloomin' obvious."

"And you're the queen of telling me so. Now, what say we go inside and get a late lunch?" Horace chortled.

Marjorie turned to follow her two companions inside. Frederick offered her his arm as she climbed the steps, which certainly beat using her walking stick.

Marjorie lowered her voice. "I agree with Horace. That man's on some sort of dark mission. I've been mulling over our earlier conversation on the forest trail. He's here on a vendetta."

"I suggest we steer clear of him," said Frederick. "I've gone off the man after witnessing that display. Such a pleasant woman, too. I hope he doesn't put a dampener on her grand opening weeks."

"I fear he already has," said Marjorie, watching their hostess passing by with Faith in hot pursuit. "She looks like she'd like to run for the hills."

"At least there are plenty of those round here." Frederick smiled, and Marjorie appreciated his attempt at making light of the situation.

"She'd be quite within her rights to ask him to leave."

"An independent woman like that is more likely to weather whatever storm he's brought with him," said Frederick. "Besides, she appears to have a burly, albeit older, protector by her side."

"You noticed him too. He was quickly at her side. You're right; I expect he'll make sure Jock McGuire stays out of Nessa's hair."

They both turned around on reaching the top of the steps, to appreciate the vista. Marjorie watched the coach depart, carrying the rest of the tour party. It turned right at the bottom of the track. She could just make out another hotel in the distance and presumed that was where they would be staying. The view of the loch from where they stood was breathtaking, and everything was eerily quiet now the guests had gone inside. At least it was for a few welcome moments until the familiar voice shattered the peace.

"Come on, Marge. I'm starving."

Marjorie grimaced before turning to follow her cousin-in-law indoors. "You're anything but starving. Was the greasy food you devoured at breakfast not enough for you this morning?"

"That was hours ago."

"What about the four slices of toast at Manchester airport?"

"I hadn't had time to do toast with me breakfast. Too busy searching for your prunes."

"And the doughnut at Inverness airport?" Marjorie wasn't backing down.

Edna held her palms up. "Okay, okay. I'm hungry, not starving – satisfied?"

"Quite," said Marjorie, triumphantly. "I assume you've checked in?"

"No, we don't need to. Faith's going to do the rounds with room keys. Horace has already gone through to the restaurant to get us a table. I think that Mick bloke might join us. His daughter and her fiancé have gone for a wander."

"They seem very young to be engaged. I didn't see a ring."

"Maybe he's just saying it then 'cos they're sharing a room." Edna cackled. "By the way, she's twenty-four; so he says."

"I don't see why he'd lie over his daughter's age, but she doesn't look a day over eighteen," said Marjorie, trying to take in the hotel surroundings whilst being corralled into the restaurant. The other guests were milling around the reception area, with some sitting in the lobby, presumably waiting for Faith to come out of Nessa's office with their keys. Marjorie glimpsed the two women who had moved into the manager's office and could see they were locked in an earnest conversation. "I expect that's more about a certain guest than keys," she muttered.

"What are you talking about now, Marge? Sometimes I think your mind wanders. Me and Fred asked where you would like to sit. Seems we're the only group needing sustenance at the moment."

"There's nothing wrong with my mind, thank you. Hasn't Horace chosen a table? I thought you said that's what he was doing." Marjorie dragged her gaze away from the office to see a beautifully ornate, brightly lit restaurant with large brass chandeliers hanging from the ceiling. Horace was speaking to a waiter in his thirties dressed in a navy-blue tartan kilt, navy tie, and a white shirt.

Edna's jaw dropped, staring at the athletic man's knees and muscular calves protruding through the knee-high socks.

Marjorie held up a warning finger. "Not a word, Edna Parkinton, or I'm heading straight to my room."

Edna cackled before snorting. "As if I would."

"A window table overlooking the loch would be perfect." Marjorie pointed to a perfect spot, motioning to Horace.

Minutes later, the four of them were seated at a table for six. "I thought you said your new friend Mick was joining us."

"He was, but then that unpleasant fellow, McGuire, nabbed him and they went outside," Horace said. "I can't say Mick was any happier than anyone else we've seen talking to the man."

"Seems Jock McGuire wasn't joking when he said he knew a lot of people around here. Mick Burns spent a lot of time here as a child, as well as during his marriage. He told me on the way back to the car—" Frederick stopped speaking, staring goggle-eyed through the large bay window.

Marjorie turned her head to see what had grabbed his attention, as did Horace. Edna continued bemoaning strange men and expounding on how the world would be a better place without so much testosterone. She was clearly oblivious to the hormonal reactions of the two men at her own table.

"Beautiful scenery," said Horace, smirking.

"Very," agreed Frederick, grinning like a Cheshire Cat.

Edna finally cottoned on that nobody was listening to her and looked outside to see what was so interesting. Her already grumpy face formed into a deep frown as she adjusted her wig and puffed out her chest in disgust.

Chapter 7

"That's Grace Brown-Jones yer staring at. She's a sight fer sore eyes, ain't she?"

"Isn't she just," said Horace, mesmerised.

Marjorie had noticed the older man who had helped bring suitcases in from the coach and who had followed Jock McGuire into the hotel, patiently waiting for them to acknowledge his presence without success.

"The name's Brian. What can I get yer?" He clearly gave up, deciding to interrupt the men's mutual admiration society.

Reluctantly, Horace and Frederick removed their eyes from the bleached-blonde beauty called Grace Brown-Jones. Marjorie hazarded a guess that the woman was in her late forties. As well as being shaped like a goddess, she dressed to impress with a flowing red dress and a bright red Lamborghini parked next to the terrace.

"Most people go for matching shoes. That lady goes for a matching car," remarked Marjorie, chuckling.

"She has the shoes as well," said Frederick. "Is Grace Brown-Jones staying here?" he asked Brian, bald head flushing a dark shade of pink.

"Aye, she is that. She's here for the autumn stag mating season."

Marjorie didn't get the opportunity to ask why a woman dressed so elegantly would be in the Highlands for the deer mating season, because a petulant Edna had clearly had enough of the conversation. "He asked what we wanted to eat in case you hadn't noticed. I'm pretty sure he doesn't have time to stand here all day while you two gawp at the blonde."

Horace smirked, recognising Edna's envy, but was sensible enough to say nothing.

Frederick cleared his throat, looking at the waiter. "What do you recommend?"

"It depends how hungry you are. There's a nice hot Scotch broth if yer want a bit 'o meat or there's a tattie soup."

Horace and Frederick opted for the Scotch broth.

"Will yer be wanting plen brid wi it?"

Horace appeared confused.

"Plain bread," explained Frederick, pointing to the menu. "Yes, we'll have the bread with it, thank you," he said to Brian.

Edna scoured the menu with a deep frown on her face, still angry about the presence of Grace Brown-Jones outside. "Fish and chips for me," she said without enthusiasm.

Brian looked at Marjorie, smiling. The tall, muscular man had a twinkle in his deep set dark blue eyes. His weatherworn face was lined with deep wrinkles and he needed a shave. She felt her estimate that he was probably mid-seventies was accurate, but one never could tell.

"I'll have the fresh salmon salad please, Brian, and a pot of tea."

"Will that be teas all roond?" Brian asked.

"Coffee for me," said Horace. "What about you, Fred?"

Frederick's attention had returned to the window, or more specifically, *the blonde,* as Edna referred to her.

Marjorie was about to make a quip with Brian about men and attractive women when she noticed his face harden as he, too, looked out of the window. Only this time, his glower was ominous.

"Isn't that Jock McGuire?" said Frederick. "I thought you said he was with Mick?"

Marjorie turned to see Jock and the woman called Grace Brown-Jones locked in an intense conversation.

"It is Jock McGuire, and yes he was before we came in here," said Horace. "She doesn't seem pleased to see him, does she?"

"His name's nae Jock. It's Phil. Phil McGuire," said Brian. "I'd stay away from him if I was you. He's nowt but trouble." Brian gave Jock one more deathly stare before turning on his heels and heading across the restaurant with their order written on his pad.

"Jock – or should I say Phil – McGuire isn't popular around here, is he?" said Frederick.

"I think we'll stick to Jock; all too confusing otherwise. He's not a nice fella, by all accounts. I wonder why he changed his name?" Horace said.

Marjorie assumed it was so he could book onto this holiday without Vanessa Wallace realising he was coming from what they had witnessed from the stiff greeting outside. "He's here to stir up trouble from the past, I fear. If he wasn't so bitter, and slightly paranoid, I'd be intrigued."

"What makes you say he's bitter, Marge?" Edna appeared happy to talk about someone other than the woman turning their male companions' heads.

"There was a hint of something in his tone when I met him in the forest earlier, but witnessing his interactions with Vanessa and now Grace Brown-Jones, and the rather protective Brian's reaction, I suspect he really does have a story to tell."

"An Exposé, he called it," said Fred.

"Whatever he's doing here, he should leave the ladies alone," said Horace glumly.

Horace turned to look out of the window again as the object of his attention climbed into her Lamborghini. McGuire leaned down, placing his hands on the door. The blonde beauty poked him in the chest and moments later, the engine roared and she and the beautiful car were gone.

"It's not just the engine that roars," said Marjorie.

They all watched as the car tore down the lane and Marjorie added, "It's as if the driver has a pack of wolves on her tail."

"Judging by Horace and Fred's bedazzled expressions, it wouldn't surprise me if she did," snapped Edna, still put out at not being the centre of attention.

"I wonder who she is." Horace ignored the rebuke from Edna.

"Grace Brown-Jones, here for the stag season. There might be a rut inside and outside, by the looks of you two." Edna sighed.

"Whoever the woman behind the name is; she's got money to burn," said Marjorie. "I'm more concerned about what Jock McGuire was saying to her and why he's really here."

"To write a book," said Frederick.

"He could do that anywhere," said Marjorie. "It's more than that. I fear his intention is to bring a storm to this idyllic refuge."

"Maybe Nessa Wallace will turn him out," said Horace, sounding hopeful.

"I hope so 'cos I ain't letting no man ruin my holiday," said Edna.

"Perhaps the Loch Ness Monster is less of a threat now, hey?" Horace teased, patting Edna's hand.

***

Marjorie spent an hour after lunch unpacking, having familiarised herself with the hotel, and decided to take a stroll through its beautiful grounds. Edna had developed a headache during lunch, and excused herself soon afterwards to go for a sleep. As they were leaving the restaurant, Horace bumped into Mick Burns, whose daughter and probably fictional fiancé had left him to himself again. Mick and Horace retired to the bar for a drink. Frederick had then informed Marjorie he was going to see if he could have a word with Jock McGuire and ask him to dial the tension down a little. Marjorie had tried to dissuade him, feeling McGuire wasn't the kind of man who would take kindly to advice from anyone, let alone a stranger, no matter how well meaning. Frederick, though, had ignored her reasoning and, with a steely determination she admired, set off in search of the unpleasant man. She hoped Frederick wouldn't become a target. He stood much shorter and was much older than McGuire, but she was confident he would show discretion during his mission.

After leaving the hotel verandah and climbing a steep slope at a leisurely pace, Marjorie found herself in an attractive part walled, part hedged garden. Whoever maintained the grounds of Nessie's Lakeside Hotel did so with diligence, and they were also creative. She admired how the sloping banks were being managed to appear wild, and yet the land was being tamed in a way that kept it from being overrun. As she meandered through the garden, appreciating the fresh air and feeling herself relax, she inhaled the aromas from the sensory balms all around her. Pink heathers were dotted around the edges, but there were also deep red hydrangeas, hardy fuchsias, sedum and some late-flowering variegated roses still in bloom. It was the scent of the roses that made her feel so at home. She herself had a beautiful rose garden, but there were some varieties here she had never seen before.

"I'll ask to speak to the gardener," she said out loud while continuing to amble through the garden. She came to a stone wall covered with Virginia Creeper, its beautiful autumn red and orange foliage on display. Marjorie wandered through an arched entrance built into the stone wall and looked down the hillside at the beautiful loch. It was a view to die for. Goats grazed on the hillside. "Ah, that's how they keep the grass under control," she said.

"Pardon?"

Marjorie hadn't noticed a man she recognised as one half of the couple she had seen arguing with Jock McGuire by Rogie Falls earlier in the day. He was standing next to a half-full wheelbarrow.

"My apologies," she said. "I have a tendency to speak to myself and didn't realise there was anyone else here. I've been admiring how well kept the slopes are, and seeing the goats just now made it all click into place."

"They do a grand job. We also get good milk from them, but people don't like to drink it much around these parts. We have a deal with a local farm. They take the milk and turn it into cheese. We sell a bit to the posh hotel up the road – some of their customers like it in their tea. Goat's milk is sweet, so no need for sugar."

Marjorie had thought this man was part of their tour party, but he clearly worked here. "Are you responsible for the beautiful garden I've just come from?"

"That and all the rest of it. I'm the head gardener, Terry, Terry Stewart. I'd shake your hand, but mine are dirty."

Terry Stewart was mid-forties, with ruddy cheeks and an open face. Marjorie liked him instantly. She noticed he wasn't wearing gloves and his hands indeed were caked with mud. "It's a pleasure to meet you. I'm Marjorie Snellthorpe. You're not from these parts, are you?"

"The English accent gave me away then? I'm from Yorkshire, but my wife grew up in a village a couple of miles from here. We met at Edinburgh University. We tried living in Yorkshire, but the wife missed her homeland."

Majorie looked down at the loch, "I can't blame her for that."

"Me neither, to be honest. We moved back to Edinburgh for a while, but city life didn't suit either of us. I love the land. My degree was in landscape gardening, so when this job came up, it was the perfect opening for us. I've been taming the land here for the past year, getting ready for the grand opening. You should have seen it before. It was beautiful but wild."

"I suppose it gets harsh during the winter," Marjorie said.

"It did last year. But that's my favourite time. I'm a Yorkshire man at heart, always will be, but nothing beats this place in winter. And with Gemma's family still in the same village, she's happy. Gemma helps out with the rooms and does a bit of reception work."

"Do you live in the village?"

"No, we live on site. There's a cottage at the back of the hotel. I like the in-laws close, yet not too close, if you know what I mean?"

"I do." Marjorie remembered when she first married Ralph. They had lived with his parents for twelve months before buying their first home. As much as she got on with Ralph's parents, it was a challenging time. "Was that your wife I saw you with at Rogie Falls?" A flicker of a frown crossed Terry Stewart's face for a moment. "Yeah. I collected her from the airport. She'd been down to London to visit some friends she met at uni. Nessa got one of the staff to drop me off at the airport while they went shopping and told me we should cadge a lift back on the bus and visit to the falls. She loves it there."

Marjorie wondered why he hadn't driven. However, something else was preying on her mind. The argument with Jock McGuire at Rogie Falls. "Is your wife from Scraghead?"

"You've heard of it then?"

"Not before today. Did I see you and your wife in conversation with that author who comes from there, erm…"

A dark cloud gathered overhead, though not as dark as the one descending over Terry Stewart's face. His jaw twitched as he spoke through gritted teeth. "McGuire. Phil McGuire's no author. He's a troublemaker."

"Oh, forgive me. He told me his name was Jock. Perhaps we're not speaking about the same man. I must be mistaken."

"A change of name doesn't change the man. Stay away from him, Mrs Snellthorpe. According to my wife, the man's a compulsive liar and a stirrer. I wouldn't take any notice of anything he says. Now, if you'll excuse me, I'd better get on." Terry turned his wheelbarrow in the opposite direction and was out of sight before she had any time to reply.

If the grim reactions so far were anything to go by, Jock-AKA-Phil McGuire might not have been exaggerating when he warned her someone might try to kill him. That was an overreaction, surely?

Chapter 8

Edna's head told her she was overreacting, but her pounding heart said otherwise. She couldn't shake off the feeling that something terrible was going to happen. Now Marge had seen through her earlier bravado, she wondered if it would be best to give up and go home. The belief that something large and terrifying was brooding beneath the deep waters of the loch filled her with an irrational dread. She had barely slept despite taking a couple of paracetamol for her headache. It was awful being in a room on her own overlooking the place, giving her the heebie-jeebies.

"Why are you reacting like this, Parkinton? You know it doesn't make any sense." Frustration with herself quelled the terror a fraction. Deep down in the recesses of her brain, she realised the fear went way back. As a child, Edna had suffered terrifying nightmares filled with monsters and ogres shortly after her dad left home. Edna's mam did her best to reassure her, but with her mam working late nights as a singer, her brother reinforced – even added to – her terror by telling her stories of ghouls and bogeymen. He hadn't meant to cause her harm, he was just teasing, but it left her suffering petrified nights alone in her room until she finally heard the reassuring turn of the key in the lock when her mam come home. Edna had grown out of the nightmares, of course, but since arriving here, the anxiety and lack of confidence had returned. It wasn't easy to talk about this to anyone, especially not Marge, who was always in control.

"Be rational," Horace had cajoled her this morning. "Even if the monster exists, it's hardly going to come to the hotel, is it?"

She had laughed. It was easy to laugh in the comfort and presence of others. But now she was in a room on her own, it resurrected the small child with all her foreboding collywobbles. Edna felt isolated. What was worse, there was no mobile phone signal. She picked up the hotel information folder and leafed through. A page spelled out that in some parts of the hotel there was a blind spot for mobile phones. Internet could also be intermittent, it read.

"You've got that right," she groaned. "Just flippin' great!"

After taking a speedy shower, Edna dressed in the same clothes she had taken off, not wanting to spend any more time in the room on her own than necessary. She also decided not to unpack just yet, just in case. The only items she had removed from her suitcase were her wash bag and her wigs. The wigs had to be nurtured. She picked up the blonde one, replacing the redhead that had seen her through the day.

Tonight, she needed something special. "I'll show that blonde what's what," she muttered, admiring her reflection in the mirror. "You're still a looker, you know, Edna."

After donning her new wig, she added a quick layer of lipstick before readjusting her hair — these readjustments always gave her confidence – she dashed out, closing the door and leaving her inner demons behind.

There was no reply from Marjorie's room when she knocked. Edna inhaled a deep breath, exhaling purposefully. "You can do this," she told herself.

Horace was in the bar chatting to Mick Burns, the guy with the drooling teenagers. The ever reliable, albeit old-fashioned, Horace stood to pull out a seat for her. "What are you having, Edna? Scotch?"

Edna shook her head. "I'll do a Marge and have a brandy." Her cousin believed in the power of brandy to soothe the nerves.

"Brandy it is." Horace went to the bar to buy the drink.

"Where's your daughter?" she asked Mick.

"Gone out. I shouldn't have brought them. She's a city girl through and through. I thought it would help us bond again. She's been distant of late."

"I thought you said you came here a lot with your wife?" Mick was a big man, muscular as well as overweight. He clearly had outward strength, but underneath the gruff bark, he seemed timid and lost. Having recently lost his wife, Edna understood how he might feel. It wasn't that long since she lost her Dennis. Her better half, she called him, and he was.

"We did, but that was when Shelagh was a kid. I haven't been back for many years, and now I'm here, I realise it probably wasn't such a good idea. Too many memories all round."

"I suppose you know that Jock fella if you grew up around here. Do you reckon you'll appear in his book?" Edna always spoke first, thought afterwards, but she knew immediately she'd hit a nerve.

Mick pushed back in his seat. "Why should I be? What did he say to you?"

"Nothing. I just thought with you being from these parts, you might know each other." Keep yer 'air on mate, she wanted to say, but instead said, "He seems intent on telling stories about people from his past and revealing secrets and all that. Can't say I like him though."

"I knew him but didn't *know* him, if you know what I mean. He was never my type. Always causing trouble and picking fights with kids in the village. His dad was the same, that's why he ended up—" Mick stopped speaking, stood up, grabbed his glass and downed the rest of a pint of malt.

"Ended up what?"

"I need to find Shelagh and Kevin."

"What was that all about?" Horace had arrived during the latter part of the conversation. He handed Edna a brandy.

Edna shrugged. "I only asked him if he thought he would feature in that McGuire bloke's book, and he went off on one. Well, sort of did. I think he's scared he's gonna be in the book. Seems they've all got something to hide around here. One minute he swore he hardly knew the man, and the next he told me he was always trouble."

"I thought I heard him mention Jock's father?" Horace took a sip from his freshly filled pint glass.

"Yeah, he implied something happened to the dad but didn't say what. That's when he stormed off in a bit of a huff. If you ask me, he's got some skeletons in the cupboard."

Horace grinned, a mischievous twinkle in his eye. "We all have things we'd rather people didn't know about, Edna. I suspect even Lady Marjorie has the odd secret, eh?"

Edna loved Horace's cheerful disposition, which generally matched her own, except for days like today. "I wouldn't know. I doubt it. She reminds me of Saint Teresa.

Perfect in every way. Me now, that's something else." It was her turn to grin.

"Let's drink to that," said Horace. "Where is the indomitable Lady Marjorie, by the way?"

Edna felt the gloom-cloud building up again. "I don't know. She's not in her room. I wish she wouldn't wander off on her own, especially not round here."

"Don't start with that nonsense again. The only monster in these parts is Jock McGuire. I don't like him upsetting the ladies."

"What about the men?"

"Men can take care of themselves, in my opinion."

"I've said it before and I'll say it again. Horace Tyler: you're a dinosaur."

Horace snorted with laughter, and she couldn't help but cackle. "Maybe Marge's with Fred," she smirked.

"I'm afraid not. I saw him talking to the man in question, Jock McGuire, about an hour ago. They came in from outside. Jock hung around reception for a while, most probably hoping to annoy Nessa, but she's made herself scarce all afternoon. I haven't seen her."

"Who can blame her? I bet she needed a lie down after seeing him. Why was Fred talking to the man? I don't want him joining our crew."

"Me neither. I like Mick, but I don't want any more to do with Mr McGuire."

They sat chatting while Horace finished his pint, then, looking at his watch, he said, "I'd better go upstairs and change for dinner. Are you going up?"

"No, I'll wait for Marjorie to come back."

"Shall we meet back here in an hour?"

"Suits me. I'll tell Marjorie. I would imagine she'll turn up soon."

"I'll give Fred a knock on my way up and tell him the plan. Nice wig, by the way," Horace winked before heading for the stairs. Unlike her, he preferred to get as much exercise as possible.

Edna stared into the brandy glass for what seemed like an age before she spotted Marjorie entering the lobby. An enormous sense of relief ran through her. She left the brandy, half drunk, and rushed over.

Chapter 9

"There you are, Marge. I've been looking everywhere for you. You really shouldn't go off by yourself without telling anyone where you're going. I almost got up a search party."

Marjorie stopped herself from rebuking her cousin-in-law when she noted the genuine look of concern in Edna's eyes. She was afraid of something, and it was clearly making her nervous. It had astonished Marjorie to learn Edna believed in the Loch Ness Monster, but even if she did, how could the crazed woman imagine it would turn up on the shores close to their hotel?

"I was exploring the grounds. There's a beautiful garden, and I met the head gardener; his name's Terry. He and his wife were at Rogie Falls. How's your headache?"

"Almost gone now, thanks. I've just seen Horace. He suggested we meet him and Fred for dinner in an hour."

"I'd better wash and change then. It's been rather a long day, so I'll be pleased to eat soon and get an early night."

"Right you are, Marge. I'll wait in the bar."

"Aren't you dressing for dinner?" Marjorie asked.

"Nah. Can't be bothered. I took a shower after I woke up, though, and changed me wig. You didn't notice, did you?" Edna adjusted the shoulder-length blonde headpiece.

"I think you'll find it hard to compete with Grace Brown-Jones if that's what you're up to," Marjorie laughed.

"Who? Oh, you mean the rich blonde? I hadn't given her a thought."

Of course not, Marjorie thought, but replied. "I'll see you in an hour, then."

Marjorie returned to her room and took a closer look around. She had hurriedly unpacked before going out for some fresh air. The need to explore the hotel and its grounds was more inviting than being stuck inside a hotel room. The smell of lavender was the first thing that struck her. She was certain it hadn't been there earlier. The odour filled the bedroom, filtering from a ceramic container filled with potpourri in the bathroom. The bedroom itself was roomy. A king-sized bed was covered with a heavy duvet and covered by a purple patterned bedspread. Seeing the bed made her feel tired, so she cast her eyes elsewhere. The smell of fresh paint lingered in the air, which explained the need for a heavy dose of lavender. Before taking a shower, she was pleased to find hers was one room with a bathtub.

"Faith's doing, no doubt."

Marjorie hummed while dressing until a sudden roll of thunder and driving rain tumbled in via the window she'd opened earlier. She rushed over to close it as a flash of lightning drew her attention towards the shadow of a man walking alone in the distance.

"A local, I suspect." The distinct sound of the Lamborghini's engine and the glare from bright headlights coming up the drive forced her back a few paces. She pulled the blind and returned to the bedroom to dress for dinner.

***

Edna and Horace were waiting in the bar by the time Marjorie arrived. There was no sign of Frederick.

"Fred's gone upstairs to change," said Edna, as if reading her mind. "Horace thought he'd be in his room but it turned out he'd gone for another walk. I don't do all this walking or the dressing for dinner nonsense."

"Except in the hair department," Marjorie quipped, ignoring the reference to Frederick.

Edna's hands leapt to her head in her wig's defence. "That's different. A lady's hair should always look immaculate. You know that."

"Quite," said Marjorie.

"But not every woman has so many styles and colours to choose from," teased Horace.

Edna took his comment in good humour with both of them snorting in unison. It was good to see her cousin-in-law relaxing again. She had been unusually glum since they'd arrived at the hotel. Perhaps the headache was still bothering her. Marjorie found it difficult to believe it could really have anything to do with Edna's notion of the existence of the Loch Ness Monster.

"Would you like an apéritif, Marjorie?" Horace asked.

"Not tonight, thank you. I'll settle for wine with dinner and an early night."

"In that case, let's go in. I told Fred we'd order for him. He chose what he wanted to eat before going upstairs and said he wouldn't be long."

Brian was on duty again and nodded curtly as they chose the same table from this afternoon.

"What is it about the security one finds in choosing the same table and seats wherever one goes?" Marjorie asked, not expecting an answer, but she got one anyway.

"Exactly that," said Edna. "Security… It starts at school and continues throughout life."

Marjorie felt it started before school. Her mother and father always sat in the same chair long before she began her education and she had a favourite cushion; one of her earliest memories.

The thunder and lightning had stopped, but the rain continued pounding against the windows, albeit muffled behind heavy curtains Brian pulled across once they were seated. "We've got triple glazing, but closing these helps keep the warmth in," he explained. "Will the other fella be joining yer?"

"Yes, he was soaking wet when he got in. We have his permission to order, so there's no need to wait. It's been rather a long day for the ladies," Horace explained.

"Not to mention the men," said Edna, never one to let Horace's sexism – in her opinion – pass without comment. Marjorie felt Horace was one of a dying breed of chivalrous gentlemen, even though he could be a show-off and a flirt.

They ordered drinks, and by the time the wine arrived, so had Frederick.

"Sorry to be late. I got drenched. The storm came on so quickly, it took me by surprise."

"Did you have a pleasant stroll?" Marjorie wanted to ask if he had spoken to Jock McGuire after lunch, but felt it polite to ask about his outing first.

"Most invigorating. The views and grounds are spectacular."

Brian reappeared to take food orders, delaying the opportunity to ask whether he had met with McGuire.

Not quite ready to sample haggis, Marjorie opted for a Scots Pheasant stew. Edna chose a beef stew, and both men chose venison.

Marjorie glanced around the restaurant. There were a few others dining, but none of the people they had seen or met during the day. "It's quiet in here, considering the place is fully booked," she said.

"We're early, Marge. Most people won't eat until after seven."

"Yes. I suppose you're quite right. I forget that when one's on holiday, one eats a little later than usual."

The food arrived before Marjorie could ask Frederick about Jock McGuire because Edna had been telling her and Frederick about a conversation she'd had with Mick Burns. Marjorie didn't want to stop her, finding the effect Jock seemed to have on so many people interesting and disturbing in equal measure. When Edna finished, Marjorie took her chance and asked Frederick.

"Did you have any success speaking to the aforementioned troublemaker this afternoon?"

"Yeah, Horace said you came in with him earlier. Why would you waste time talking to him?" asked Edna.

"Frederick didn't like the way Jock McGuire was upsetting everyone and chose to have a quiet word," Marjorie explained.

"Why didn't I know about this?" Edna snapped.

"Because you went to bed with a headache and I haven't asked about it until now. If it helps, Horace didn't know the reason either, and he's not pouting. Now, please, may we allow Frederic to answer?" Edna could be so exasperating. This was turning into one of those occasions.

"Yes, let the man speak, Edna." Horace had a way of keeping Edna under control without offending her, an art she herself hadn't managed to acquire.

"I did have a word, actually. He was reasonably amenable about it, as a matter of fact; a little taken aback by my approach, but he'll be leaving in the morning. He told me he'd said all he had to say to the people concerned and didn't feel the need to stay any longer. He appeared nervous and rattled now I think about it."

"Well, ain't that a turnup," said Edna. "I was expecting you to say he told you to mind your own business."

"He did so at first, but when I explained why I was concerned, he changed his tune. Either that or he was fobbing me off. His demeanour changed when he spotted someone behind me. That's when his eyes widened. I'd say he was frightened of whoever it was."

"Who was it?" asked Marjorie.

"I didn't see the person. When I asked him about it, he denied seeing anyone, but I'm almost certain there was. Either that, or he saw something else that bothered him."

"Which way was he looking?" The colour drained from Edna's face.

"Down towards the loch. I couldn't turn quickly enough because I was on a slope and it was hard to keep my footing. It might have been no-one, but he definitely changed tack afterwards. That's when he told me he had done what he set out to do and would leave us holidaymakers alone."

"He saw the monster…" Edna's trembling words couldn't finish the sentence.

"Don't be ridiculous," said Frederick. "There is no monster. If he saw anything at all, it was a person."

"Since when did you become such an expert on the Loch Ness Monster?" Edna snapped. "You said you didn't see anyone, so it could have been the monster."

Horace poured Edna another glass of wine and patted her arm. "If the monster had put in an appearance this afternoon, news would have travelled all around the hotel and the press would be banging at the door. Trust me, Edna; you're quite safe."

"Well, I for one am pleased McGuire's leaving," said Marjorie. "He's had a detrimental influence over far too many people in a short space of time. Whatever he wants to write about, let him go away and do it elsewhere."

"That's another thing," said Frederick. "He told me he'd almost finished the book and had a malicious glint in his eye when he said he just needed to add a few last details following his conversations today. He took my address, said he'd send me a signed copy."

"Bully for you," said Edna. "Although I wouldn't mind having a read when you've finished like. I enjoy a bit of gossip."

"I thought you didn't like the man?" Horace chuckled.

"I don't, but that doesn't mean I wouldn't want to hear what this lot got up to in the past. Especially the blonde. I'm sure she'll take centre stage in his book."

Marjorie noticed both Horace and Frederick's cheeks blushing at the mention of the attractive woman, Grace Brown-Jones, whom they had seen earlier.

"I was hoping to catch a word with said *blonde* this evening," said Horace. Never one to miss the opportunity of making his intentions clear. "I asked Mick about her. She's a landowner in these parts."

"Interested in investing, are we?" Edna spat sarcasm.

"No, but I am interested in stags and does," he winked. "If you get my meaning."

Missing the point, Frederick said. "So am I. They're wonderful creatures. I might join you if she comes in."

"The two of you are so bloomin' obvious," Edna complained. "Why don't you admit you want to chat her up?"

"If the opportunity arises, I won't deny I'd certainly be interested," said Horace.

Frederick said nothing, but from the hopeful look in his eyes, Marjorie guessed he, too, was interested. She hoped it was a passing fad, preferring the four of them to continue to be holiday companions. She told herself it was nothing more than that.

"You're both too old for her anyway, and you should be careful what you wish for, Horace Tyler. I bet Grace Brown-Jones eats men like you for breakfast," said Edna.

"I'm counting on it," said Horace, winking again.

Ignoring him, Edna continued. "Besides which, I can't see what's so interesting apart from the car."

"That's because you're not a man," said Horace, with a wide grin on his face.

With dinner over, Faith appeared at an opportune moment before Horace tempted Edna to say something she might later regret. "I'm just confirming numbers and time for the Loch Ness boat tour tomorrow. The captain's been in touch and tells me the tides are suitable for us to leave at eight-thirty. I take it you'll all be joining us?" Faith's eyes were aglow with excitement. Queen Cruises, it seemed, was expanding in every way possible, even stretching to chartering boats that weren't their own.

"Absolutely. Count us in," said Horace.

Marjorie caught a glimmer of hesitation cross Edna's face as she opened and closed her mouth.

"I'm very much looking forward to it," said Frederick.

Faith ticked their names off on her trusty clipboard. "Wonderful. I think that's almost everyone. I hope you don't mind, but Nessa asked if we'd take another guest who's staying at the hotel."

Edna visibly stiffened. "Who?"

"A Mrs Brown-Jones."

"Mrs, you say…" Edna smirked before giving Horace a 'how about that?' look.

"Will her husband be coming along too?" Horace grinned back at Edna.

"I don't believe he's with her… Do you know the lady?" Faith's forehead creased.

"Not yet," said Horace, "but we've seen her."

"And her Lamborghini." Edna puffed out her cheeks as she blew a breath through pursed lips.

"Oh?" Faith nodded, only half-listening, concentrating on the list once more. "I'd better find Mr McGuire. He's the only one who hasn't confirmed the trip. Have any of you seen him?"

"Not recently. Can't say I want to either," said Horace.

"Fred was the last to see him," said Edna.

"He said he was going for a drink after I finished speaking to him this afternoon."

"Oh yes, I saw him hanging about in the bar for a bit, then he went out again," said Horace.

"Now I think of it, I think I saw a shadow that looked like him walking along the shore during the storm," said Marjorie, suddenly remembering the beard had been lit up by the lightning.

"I don't think he'll be coming with us, anyway. He told me he would check out tomorrow morning," Frederick added.

"Really?" Faith sounded unusually hopeful that one of the tour guests would be leaving so soon after the holiday had started. Marjorie suspected Vanessa Wallace had shared something of her concerns – if she had any – with their discreet tour guide. "That's settled then. I'll confirm numbers with Captain Sturgeon."

"Sturgeon?" Horace raised both colour tinted eyebrows.

"You've got to be kidding me," said Edna.

"I bet that's not his real name… glorious name for a ship's captain, though," added Marjorie.

Horace guffawed. Edna joined in with Horace's laughter, but not with her usual vigour. There was no snorting for once. Was it fear of running into Nessie, or the fact that Grace Brown-Jones would spend the day with them? No doubt, it would soon be revealed. Frederick, on the other hand, was beaming.

Chapter 10

A thick, drizzly morning mist hung low over the water. The eerie mists around the loch were one thing Jock McGuire had loved when growing up. It was the first time he'd been back in the area for thirty years, and it amazed him how little had changed. And yet, lots of things looked different from the outside. These external changes were cosmetic at best, merely superficial, like painting over cracks. Underneath all the pretence, just like the unseen dangers from the currents in the depths of the loch, there lurked secrets no-one spoke about. These remained hidden… unmentionable. Not for much longer, eh? He was about to throw the doors wide open and tell the world about his enemies. They might pretend to forget, but he would not rest until he'd exposed them for what they were. Jock clenched determined fists inside his coat pockets, walking faster.

"You'll be sorry," he muttered, then yelled, "YOU'LL ALL BE SORRY." His shouts disappeared into the gloom. He almost expected a reply as his voice echoed back at him, haunting. He laughed loudly, that too echoing in the quiet morning. Then it was silent again, except for a regular gurgling from the water hitting the pebbled shore.

Last night Jock had returned to the village where he'd grown up, just to show them he wasn't afraid anymore. He had seen no-one. The inhabitants had remained inside their homes, but he'd felt the twitching of curtains and hidden, watchful eyes following him down the main road until he came to a standstill outside of his childhood home. His ma had long since died, putting up a good fight against the hypocritical neighbours. The house remained empty, which was how he had wanted it to stay. A reminder to these sanctimonious pretenders of what they had done all those years ago. Jock peered through the curtainless front window. The heavy rain hammering against it had stung his eyes. Or were those his own tears? It was hard to tell as the two had mingled into one. He remembered fiddling with the house keys in his trouser pocket, deliberating, but in the end, he'd decided not to go inside the shell that was once a family, if not happy, home. Too many memories lay inside that house. He had decided there and then to drop the keys off at the estate agents this morning and let them put the house on the market. There was no point hanging onto the place any longer. It was time to let it go, just like he'd let his old name go. He'd enjoyed the look of surprise on Nessa's face when she saw him. He wondered whether to taunt her some more, but nae, it wasn't worth it. She knew what he knew and soon the story itself would be enough to remind her and all the villagers, plus those he'd run into up at the hotel, the past can never be forgotten. They had their reasons for keeping it quiet and he had his for telling the world.

Jock shook painful memories from his head. This place was destroying his mind. He would never find peace here. It was time to leave. He stopped on the gravelly shore and picked up a big stone, throwing it as far as he could into the loch.

"Come on Nessie. If you're out there, you and me can create more havoc than this place has ever seen." Jock laughed again, almost hysterically.

"Nessie's Lochside Hotel!" he yelled, scornfully. "Who are you trying to kid? The lot of yer." He turned his back on the water, glaring up at the shadow of her hotel nestled in the hill, rage overwhelming him. "No-one will want to come here after my book's published. Do you hear me, Vanessa Devious Wallace? NO-ONE! There's no starting afresh around these parts. You should have left. I warned you to leave, but no, you stayed and kept your lapdog on. I suppose you think he can protect you and yer mates." Jock laughed, a hollow, bitter noise, even to his own ears.

"I'll make you pay. Every single one of you." Jock stopped his tirade for a few moments, turning once more to face Loch Ness before trudging further up to the new wooden path.

"Whatever it is that's bothering you…" the man, Frederick Mackworth, had said, "surely it's time to bury the past and move on."

Mackworth couldn't have spoken truer words. But burial only comes after death, his fists clenched in his pockets once more. And Jock McGuire had every intention of burying the handful he was determined to destroy. Revenge is sweet. Physical death would be too kind for that lot. He intended to make them suffer, and he'd devised a way to do it.

Frederick had said a lot of well-meaning things, but Jock's brain rejected the majority. Under different circumstances, he might have opened up. A different time, a different place. Maybe he and Frederick could have been friends. Mackworth and the old woman he obviously admired seemed like good people. Jock had been angry when he heard the old girl was a sleuth – short for busybody in his book – and had been determined to warn the old girl off. He hadn't meant to barge into her in quite the way he did, but he hoped she got the message not to interfere. He tried telling her in the forest to stay out of matters that didn't concern her. She wouldn't, of course; people like her never did. Lady Marjorie, Frederick

Mackworth had called her when he was bragging about her. Perhaps he should have enlisted their help, but no, that wouldn't do. They'd try to dissuade him, tell him to forget it, but he would ne'er forget. Following the conversation with Mackworth, Jock had to admit he'd agonised all night about whether to let it all go. Even now, as he stared back at the murky water, a part of him told him the book wouldn't bring the healing he was after; that revenge might not be the answer. Perhaps he should just turn back and wade into the cold-dark waters... do away with it all for good. A movement interrupted Jock's dark thoughts. It came from his right. A twig broke, but as he tried to turn, he felt something hard crack against his head. His thoughts as he hit the ground were the words of that old woman.

'*As the exposer of secrets, Mr McGuire, it might be you who needs to heed your own warning.*'

He recognised the shadow looming over his helpless body and prepared himself for the fatal blow. He capitulated. *Perhaps it's better this way.*

Chapter 11

Edna had felt totally miserable before falling into a restless sleep. The few hours she got could hardly be called sleep. And now, when she could have slept the morning away, she was awoken – feeling groggy – by the incessant bleating of goats. Marge had said something to her on the way upstairs the night before about a conversation with the head gardener, a bloke called Terry Stewart. He had told her they kept goats to graze the hills and keep the grasses under control. She didn't realise it meant they were right outside her bedroom window! Edna hadn't been paying much attention. Not listening was one of her failings at the best of times, but that blonde had preoccupied her mind last night and ruined her evening. As if it wasn't enough feeling sick to the stomach, dreading this morning's outing. There was no way she was going to admit to Marge just how scared she was. It wouldn't do to appear weak in her cousin's eyes.

Edna had been enjoying the evening, inwardly congratulating herself on how she was suppressing her fears when that blasted woman came in and spoiled everything. Grace Brown-Jones was so damned perfect looking. But, she wondered, would the woman be quite so attractive if she weren't so rich? Horace's eye had been well and truly turned. And as for Fred, he was pathetic; all but gushing. Marge hadn't reacted. But then she wouldn't, would she? "Always the epitome of self-control is our Marge." Still, Edna was convinced she had a soft spot for Fred, so it must bother her whether or not she showed it. Somehow, imagining Marge's discomfort made her own annoyance better. Edna chuckled, "They do say a problem shared is a problem halved."

Edna struggled to choose the right wig for the boat trip. Usually she would plump for the purple one when she needed a dose of courage, but it was probably the most loose fitting and she didn't want it being swept into the loch. She could imagine Horace's guffaws, Marge's disdain and Grace Bloomin'-Jones looking down her nose as the wind carried away the purple hair before it plopped onto the surface of the water to be drenched. Edna sniggered a bit at the vision, deciding her favourite redhead would have to do. It brought her comfort and imparted fire into her belly; something she'd be needing a lot of today.

While looking in the mirror, she imagined an image of Nessie poking her head above the water wearing the purple wig. Momentarily, she forgot her troubles and burst into a fit of giggles, with the accompanying snorting which she knew irritated Marge. Edna was still smiling when she met Horace in the lobby.

"You look happy this morning," he said.

"You know me, always the life and soul…"

"Always noticeable. I'll grant you that," he said. "By the way, that's my favourite."

"What?"

"The red hair. It suits your complexion. I never asked what colour your hair was before, erm…"

"Before it disappeared?"

"Precisely."

Sounding rueful, Edna replied. "Sandy brown, but I was a dyed brunette most of the time. I never let it go grey. Mind you, if I could have guaranteed it would be snow white like Marge's, I'd have borne my years more graciously. What about you?" Horace's hair was dyed dark brown with a matching toupee, she assumed, to hide a bald patch. Like her, he colour tinted his eyebrows.

"Pretty much as you see. I have it dyed in keeping with a favourite photo. Here, look." Horace reached into his breast pocket and pulled out a photograph of himself on a beach somewhere. The year 1977 was written in the top corner. He looked dashingly handsome in Bermuda shorts and a short-sleeved white shirt, unbuttoned at the collar.

"Not bad looking in those days," she smirked, handing the prized photo back.

"What do you mean? In those days. I like to think I'm as handsome now as I was back then, though more like a fine wine, improved with age." Horace returned the photo to his pocket, tapping his jacket afterwards. "The photo was taken in the Bahamas. I mixed business with pleasure in those days." He winked.

Edna stopped herself from quipping back about how his sons had turned out because she knew Horace regretted the extramarital affairs that had caused longstanding resentment. Instead, she laughed. "You haven't changed much then."

Horace's eyes shone when he laughed, something she liked about him. She didn't fancy him as such, but valued his friendship and didn't want the bleached blonde interfering with that.

"Have you seen *Marge* this morning?" he asked mischievously.

"Don't you start calling her that, or she'll blame me. No, I came straight down; forgot to knock. Maybe she had breakfast in her room, although why anyone would want to…" Edna shuddered.

"I quite like the rooms: they're bright, airy and offer a fine view of the—"

"Exactly," interrupted Edna.

Horace could be a right pain at times, but at least he refrained from teasing her too much about the monster. He just nodded, understanding. "Enough of that. Let's get ourselves some breakfast, shall we? I bet you're *starving*," he chuckled as he copied another of her repeat expressions and Marge's pet hates.

The bulky frame of Brian was the first thing they came across, his dour face barely greeting them as they stepped inside the restaurant. Edna was beginning to recognise others from their tour party and nodded to a few people while following Brian to their usual table. "He's built more like an all-in wrestler than a waiter," she whispered to Horace.

Horace wasn't paying her any attention. His eyes were fixed elsewhere. Edna thumped him on the arm. "You're going to trip up if you're not careful."

"Pardon?"

"Brian's waiting," she hissed. "If you can take your eyes off that woman for one minute."

Horace stopped. "It's not that. Look who she's sitting with."

Edna turned her head in Grace *Pain-in-the-Neck*-Jones's direction. The woman threw her blonde mane back, laughing at something someone was saying. That someone was none other than their Fred.

"Marge's not going to like it," she said, shaking her head.

"If you don't mind, I have nae got all day." Brian's gravelly voice brought Horace to attention.

"Right you are," he grinned at the gruff man. "Don't mind us."

"I'd mind yer less if yer took yer seat, man," he growled.

Edna laughed, "That told you, Horace Tyler." She smiled at Brian. "A man who doesn't mince his words. You and me will get on fine." She patted his arm.

The corners of the waiter's eyes crinkled as he held out the chair for her. "Tea or coffee?"

"Strong coffee for me, please." Edna knew she'd won him over and parked it for future reference.

Horace responded to Brian's scowl in his direction. "Tea, please."

"I don't know how he got a job as a waiter. His people skills need a lot of work. I wouldn't get away with that behaviour in my business."

"I doubt people are lining up to be waiters in these parts. I expect the young 'uns seek work in Inverness or move south to the big cities."

"At least you got him to smile. I didn't think he had one in him. And don't think I didn't notice Edna Parkinton. You go on about me and the ladies, but you're more than a match for me in your own way."

They laughed loudly, snorting in unison. Edna had made sure she took the seat with a good view of Grace and Fred so that Horace wouldn't be too distracted.

Marge ain't gonna like it. She ain't gonna like this at all, she thought.

Chapter 12

Marjorie tiptoed quietly towards the reception desk, but discovered it was unnecessary. It appeared nobody was on duty at this early hour. The clock behind the desk registered five-thirty. Marjorie tutted.

"Anyone could come in and rob the place or murder us in our beds," she grumbled. But then, reason told her, they were in the middle of nowhere; in a place where crime was probably unheard of. "Time for an early morning stroll in the peaceful Highlands," she declared, feeling upbeat.

Moments later, she was navigating the downward track, using her walking stick for support and heading towards the misty loch. She would have invited Edna, but there were two reasons... no, three... for not doing so. The first, and probably the most important, was that the walk would be anything but peaceful if her cousin-in-law was with her. Second, Edna was not a morning person and wouldn't welcome an early awakening; she would be most likely fast asleep. And the third reason was the irrational fear Marjorie sensed in her every time Loch Ness was mentioned. Her cousin-in-law's fear was blatantly apparent the night before when Faith was confirming numbers for the boat trip. Despite Edna trying her best to hide it, the fact was she had some sort of phobia about the loch that would be difficult for her to overcome.

As Marjorie ambled further down the track, she wondered if there was any truth in the Loch Ness Monster stories. Nessie, the mythical monster was called. She recollected reading about various sightings of a prehistoric beast and had noticed some framed newspaper cuttings in the bedroom corridor which Edna had refused to look at. There had been a fair number of hoax sightings, along with others that remained unexplained. Marjorie remembered her late husband telling her about a scientific mission that had attempted to discover whether this ancient creature really presided beneath the waters. Loch Ness was the deepest lake in the United Kingdom, so it was unsurprising that it was fraught with mythical tales. Not one to dismiss the unknown lightly, Marjorie kept an open mind on most things, but somehow she couldn't believe there was a huge sea monster lurking beneath these waters not yet revealed. That said, marine biologists were discovering new species regularly. She had read recently that every year scientists discovered around 18,000 previously unknown species;

however, none were anywhere near the size of the reputed Nessie. Such creatures must have incredible survival instincts.

Deciding her time would be better spent concentrating on the path in front of her as the mist got thicker, Marjorie removed and switched on a small torch she carried in her handbag for emergencies. She hadn't remembered to put her mobile phone in the bag. Her inner critic mocked. 'It's a pity you don't carry your mobile in case of an emergency. You can't call for help with a torch!'

Dismissing such thoughts, Marjorie shrugged, "The literature in the hotel stated the signal wasn't any good around here anyway, so there's no point going back for it now. Besides, I haven't charged it for ages. The battery will be flat." Marjorie's son, Jeremy, constantly berated her for not keeping it with her at all times and, if he knew she hardly ever remembered to charge it, his ire would know no bounds. He had won the argument, if not the war, in that she packed it whenever she went away. She just couldn't bring herself to add the weighty thing to the items she considered vital which she carried in her handbag. She hadn't dared mention the phone's weight to Jeremy when he was giving her a pre-holiday lecture for fear he would bring up the smartphone topic again. The last time he had suggested she buy such a phone, he had pulled his own from his pocket, showing her how much it could do, none of which held any interest for her. She had glazed over.

Marjorie didn't consider herself anti-technology; she used a computer, could email and her internet knowledge was average, meaning she could do a Google search when required. It was just, at her age, she didn't feel the need to be available twenty-four hours a day. Besides, the whole point of a holiday was to get away from the hustle and bustle of daily life. Not that there was much hustle and bustle to hers, although she kept an eye on the business accounts to make sure Jeremy wasn't getting the company into debt.

Marjorie shook her head, chortling at the thought of what he would say if he knew what she was up to this morning. On a more serious note, she didn't want or need the latest and greatest plaything. Her son was extravagant enough for the both of them, but his wife was even more so. Jeremy was overspending again. She could tell that from his mood. He was always bad tempered, but his wrath was worse when he was building up the courage to ask her for money. Marjorie had a controlling interest in her late husband's company and, although Jeremy managed it, there was only so much he could take without her and the rest of the board knowing. His salary plus an additional personal allowance from her were generous, bordering on huge for most people, but somehow, for Jeremy, it was never enough.

By the time Marjorie repelled these worries from her head, she had reached the gates where the coach had turned off the main road the day before. Thankful she had put on sturdy shoes, she crossed the road and followed the gravel path to the edge of the shore where she slowed. The screeching of an owl as it hunted in the last throes of night broke through the silence other than the gentle lapping of the loch on the shore. She could barely see a few inches ahead of her. "This must be what they call a Scotch Mist," she said, keeping the torch pointed at the ground immediately ahead.

After teetering along the water's stony edge for a while, Marjorie decided it would be better to make for more stable ground, particularly when she almost turned her ankle over. Her stick saved her from falling. The heavy rain had left mud tracks where the gravel stopped suddenly as she headed to higher ground where the mist was less dense. Here, there was a grassy track edged by a woodland area, most likely one reason Nessa factored in when choosing the plot on which to build her beautiful hotel. Marjorie moved off the wild grasses to prevent her feet from sinking in the mud and stepped onto a solid wooden path, which made it much easier to keep her footing. After strolling slowly for a while, the mist began to clear even more, and her visibility increased enough to switch off the torch. The grey clouds allowed a three-quarter moon to shine through, which reflected on the lake where the dissipating mist allowed the light to penetrate. Marjorie was considering turning back when she heard the unmistakeable roar of Grace Brown-Jones's Lamborghini heading off from somewhere nearby. Then, she stopped suddenly on hearing rustling coming from the trees ahead of her. She hoped it wasn't Jock McGuire about to give her another warning. Marjorie turned on the torch again.

With knees feeling like sponges, she called out. "Hello! Is someone there?"

No reply.

Marjorie didn't move. With her heart pounding, her ears were on high alert. The only sound she heard was the bleating of goats in the distance. *It must have been the breeze,* she told herself. Early morning light broke through the dawn and birds began their dawn chorus, slowly building it up to a crescendo. With tremors wracking through her body, Marjorie couldn't shake away the sense she was being watched. She shuddered. Running was not an option, but if she could control her wobbly knees, it was time to leave. "You're imagining things, Snellthorpe. It's that Edna and Jock McGuire making you paranoid." Marjorie held her chest on hearing the welcome sound of footsteps heading in her direction. At that moment, she saw a crumpled heap just ahead of her. Hurrying towards the muddied boots about thirty yards away, Marjorie could see someone had fallen.

"Good heavens! It must be one of the guests. Now I wish I'd brought the wretched phone along with me." She arrived at the spot to find a pair of skinny legs protruding onto the path. Marjorie called out to whoever was marching in her direction.

"We need help! Someone has—" her words hung in the air. She gasped when daylight showed Jock McGuire's lifeless eyes staring up at the sky, his forehead crinkled as if confused by the fall. The side of his head appeared to have smashed against a large rock. The bloodstained boulder was obviously what caused his demise.

Marjorie leant down, placing trembling fingers to the man's neck.

The footsteps approached at a pace.

"What happened? Is he…?" Mick Burns knelt down, also feeling for a pulse before pounding on Jock's chest.

"I'm afraid it's too late for that," said Marjorie. "He's quite dead."

The heavens opened and rain poured down again.

Chapter 13

Once Mick stopped his hopeless attempt at resuscitation, he insisted Marjorie return to the hotel. The rain had quickly turned torrential, and the water soon washed the blood away from the boulder next to the late Jock McGuire. Marjorie tried again to use Mick's phone to call for help, but there was no signal. She had thought most modern mobiles had a facility to call for the emergency services even when out of range, but Mick's was almost as ancient as hers. Marjorie was only too happy to leave the grisly scene, particularly now the driving rain was penetrating her woollen coat. She could barely see anything, and her cheeks stung as the heavy raindrops flew at her like missiles.

"You go on ahead. You'll be much quicker without me." Marjorie couldn't keep up with Mick and was struggling to keep her footing. She wanted him to run on and call for the emergency services, but he seemed in no rush.

"I'm nae leaving you here. You might fall like he did. Anyway, there's no hurry, he's going nowhere." Mick slowed down, taking Marjorie's free arm to help her negotiate the wooden path, which was becoming increasingly slippery. They reached the road and crossed over to the sign for Nessie's. Marjorie was relieved to hear the distinctive roar of Grace Brown-Jones's Lamborghini approaching through the pounding rain.

Mick stood in the road and hailed the red sports car. Grace slammed on the brakes, bringing the car to a screeching halt.

She really should slow down in this weather, thought Marjorie.

Grace wound down her window. "What are you doing? I could have killed you!"

"Yer should nae drive so fast in this," Mick said, waving his arm at the rain.

Grace responded with an eye roll. "Men just don't like women driving. You all think we should be slaving over a hot stove and drive nothing faster than a Mini."

"This man thinks yer might kill yerself one of these days."

Marjorie couldn't agree more but said nothing.

"Well, now you've got my attention, the pair of you look drenched. I suppose you need a lift?"

Mick explained what had happened and how they had found a man dead. Marjorie thought it interesting he didn't tell her who it was, nor did she ask. "Can you drive Lady Marjorie up to the hotel and call for an ambulance? We cannae get a signal down here. There's nothing more we can do for the bloke, but I'll go back and wait with the body until the paramedics get here."

Grace Brown-Jones nodded. "Jump in," she said to Marjorie.

"My jumping days are over, I fear," said Marjorie, astonished at the woman's disinterest. It's not like they came across a body every day. Or was it?

Mick opened the car door and Marjorie somehow clambered into the low seat, thankful on this occasion for being short in stature. Once in the car, Grace tore up the track leading to the hotel. "The weather can change quickly round here. You're lucky you didn't have an accident yourself. Were you with the man who fell?"

"No. I found him lying on the ground. I recognised him though. It's a man we met yesterday. Jock McGuire, I think you knew him."

Grace turned to look at Marjorie as she brought the car to another unnecessarily screeching stop at the foot of the hotel steps. It must have excellent brakes, Marjorie thought. She felt certain it would have hit the wall otherwise.

"And he fell, you say?"

"It certainly looked that way, but I think we should call the police as well as an ambulance. I expect they will want to examine the scene just in case."

"Right," said Grace, still not moving. She appeared to be mulling something over, digesting the information. Marjorie could almost see the cogs turning; a man she had argued with the day before was now dead. Then a look of relief replaced any confusion and Grace Brown-Jones leapt out of the car, hurried around to the passenger side with an open umbrella. She opened the door for Marjorie to get out then handed her the brolly. "Take this. I'll go inside and make the calls. You'd better get in and out of those wet clothes."

A gust of wind caught the umbrella and nearly took Marjorie with it. With visions of being carried into the hills by the wretched thing, she let it down. There was not much point in using it when it was likely to do her a mischief and she was already soaking wet.

After negotiating the wet steps, Marjorie entered the hotel and felt the welcoming warmth as soon as the door closed behind her. Grace, Nessa, and Brian were having a quiet but earnest conversation. The latter never seemed to have any time off. He frowned, but that was nothing new. None of them seemed in any hurry to summon help unless they'd already done so. Either way, Jock was dead, so it wasn't necessary to prod them. Whether or not they liked the man, his death must have come as a shock, especially as he was a guest in Nessa's new hotel.

The thought struck Marjorie. There was a killer involved in Jock McGuire's death. Now she was over the shock of finding him like that, the more she mulled over the scene, the more she remembered. The position of the body and the wound to the side of his head weren't natural. She felt the death wouldn't turn out to be the result of a fall. There were also his words from the day before. They made it even more likely to be foul play. What had he said? *"It wouldn't surprise me if someone tried to kill me. If they succeed, you might get to put your sleuthing skills to the test."* Marjorie straightened. They were dealing with another murder.

Nessa caught her eye and immediately sprang into action, heading in Marjorie's direction while dishing out instructions.

"Brian, call an ambulance and the police. Tell them where Mick is… thanks Grace for your help… let's try to keep all of this between us for now. I don't want to alarm the guests. You know how slippery that path can get. We've done our best to keep it in good shape, but there's been so much rain lately."

"It's not our responsibility," growled Brian.

"Nevertheless, I feel responsible. Terry's been down there most days, removing moss and washing away slime. I never imagined something like this would happen."

Nessa had gone into overdrive; words tumbling out of her mouth.

"Is there anyone else we need to inform?" Grace called back, while Nessa continued muttering less audibly. "Any next of kin?"

"Oh, I hadn't thought of that. No-one I know, but I'll ask Faith if he listed one with her. She can let the police know when they get here. Somehow, I doubt there'll be anyone." Nessa took Marjorie's arm, transferring her manic attention to her. "You've had quite a shock, Lady Snellthorpe. Do you need me to help you to your room?"

"No thank you, I'll manage. I realise you're busy, but would you mind having a pot of tea sent up when you have a minute? I'm afraid I used all the teabags last night." *All* was an overstatement. Marjorie had felt it remiss that whoever serviced the rooms had only left two teabags next to the abundant supply of coffee sachets. Why don't they realise there are still tea drinkers in the world?

"Of course, you must be frozen. I'll get it myself. You go on up. I won't be a minute."

Nessa was true to her word and arrived whilst Marjorie was getting out of her wet clothes. Thankfully, her coat had protected most of her top half, leaving her cardigan damp but not sodden. Nessa put a tray of tea on her table, asking if Marjorie was all right and informing her an ambulance was on its way. "We've also called our local police officer."

Marjorie wanted to ask more questions, but Nessa was in a flurry of adrenaline-fuelled activity. There was no time to talk, so she put on a dressing gown and supped the welcome hot tea while the bath was filling. She made good use of the bathtub, allowing the hot water to restore the feeling in her numb extremities.

Once dressed, Marjorie stood at the window overlooking the loch with binoculars in hand. She couldn't see the exact spot where the body of Jock McGuire lay, but she noted an ambulance leaving and two police cars arriving. Presumably they had come from Inverness. "Ah good. The local bobby realises the death's suspicious. At least that means I don't have to try to persuade them." Marjorie poured a third cup of tea, which was now lukewarm, and returned to the window. She saw a black car and a white van driving slowly along the gravelled shore next to the path she had taken. Satisfied the police were taking the matter seriously and a forensic team had arrived, Marjorie felt suddenly hungry and in need of company.

Chapter 14

Edna and Horace were finishing breakfast when the steadfast Brian – behaving as though nothing had happened – showed Marjorie to their table. He gently pulled back the chair and made sure she was comfortable.

"I'll get yer a pot of tea," he said.

"What's got into him?" Horace asked, "He's been grumpy with everyone this morning."

"Except for me. I got a half-smile, remember?" Edna said before turning to Marjorie. "I thought you'd slept in and treated yourself to breakfast in bed. Faith's not long been over and told us the boat trip's been delayed by a couple of hours."

"Did she say why?"

"No, she was too busy rushing around trying to find everyone. She looked stressed out of her head. I expect the rain's affected the tide or something. Who knows? They might have to cancel it altogether," Edna said, bright eyed.

Brian appeared at the table with a full pot of tea and a pot of coffee for Edna. "I thought you might need this," he winked at Edna. "It'll be a hearty porridge for you, Lady Snellthorpe, then a fried breakfast wi' potato scones."

"Thank you, Brian. I do feel rather hungry." Marjorie felt it would be churlish to argue when the man was being so kind. "I'll have it without the black pudding, if you don't mind?"

"Not at all. I never touch the stuff myself."

Horace was watching the scene with a furrowed brow. "I wouldn't mind some tea myself if you could spare a minute."

"Aye all right," Brian replied before leaning down and whispering in Marjorie's ear. "The police have given us a bell. They'll be wanting to speak to yer later."

"Thank you, Brian."

"Nay problem. Anything else for you?" he snapped at Horace.

"Just tea, thanks."

Brian left them with Marjorie pouring her tea.

"He doesn't like men," Horace complained. "He's downright rude. I should make a complaint."

"Oh, get over yourself, Horace. He's all right," said Edna. Then turning to Marjorie, she said. "Did he just say police?" Edna could miss an entire conversation when not paying attention, but there was no doubt her hearing was acute and she hadn't missed a thing. "What have you been up to, Marge?"

Marjorie was about to explain when she noticed Frederick and Grace getting up from a table nearby. They shared what appeared to be a secret word before Grace left. Frederick nonchalantly strolled over to them, sporting a wide grin.

"Good morning," he said, taking the seat next to Horace.

"Look who's joined us at last," said Edna. "You needn't look so smug. She's just stringing you along."

Frederick straightened a grey silk tie which, as usual, didn't match his blue checked shirt. Somehow, though, the mismatch suited him. Marjorie couldn't help wondering how he and Grace had come to be having breakfast together. After the morning she'd had, it made it seem worse somehow that he had been enjoying himself whilst she had found a body, had a near-death experience in Grace's car and got drenched. Marjorie felt emotional, but swallowed hard, hearing her doctor's voice inside her head.

"Whatever you do, Marjorie, stay out of the cold and wet for at least a year. Your lung needs time to recover." Shrugging the thought away, she put it down to one of those occasions where it was not possible to shut the stable door metaphorically after the horse had bolted. Instead, she took another sip of hot tea.

"How come you got in there so fast?" Horace quizzed Frederick, eyes narrowed.

"If you're referring to my having breakfast with Grace, I didn't get in anywhere. She was upset. I asked if there was anything I could do to help and we got talking. Then we ended up having breakfast together, that's all." The glint in his eye told Marjorie he was enjoying the oneupmanship of Horace. He had the upper hand just now. One-nil, she thought to herself.

"I wouldn't have said she was upset when we came in," said Edna scornfully. "Quite the opposite, in fact." Her eyes were challenging. "You were giggling and laughing like a pair of hyenas."

Frederick stroked his chin. "Oh, that… I cheered her up a bit. It seems we have a lot in common. As well as being a wealthy landowner, she and her husband own a pharmacy chain in Scotland. We got to talking about customers and I was telling her about a woman who used to come into my chemist's shop demanding bleach to treat her leg ulcers."

Edna's eyes widened. "What on earth?"

Marjorie chuckled. "And you told her she was in the wrong shop, I take it?"

Frederick laughed, eyes dancing in the chandelier's light above the table. "Not just that. At first I tried to explain the damage she could do to her legs if she used the stuff on them. Tried to offer her alternatives, but she wouldn't have it. She came in every week asking for the same thing."

"She obviously didn't do herself too much harm," said Marjorie.

"Lucky for her, she was forgetful. I don't think she remembered to buy bleach from anywhere else, but because she associated the pharmacy with pills and potions, she assumed we would sell her misguided treatment. In the end, I had a word with the local district nurse who used to pop in to collect dressings for her patients. Good job I did, because Mrs Haydn, that was the woman's name, had finally got a bottle of bleach from somewhere, poured the lot in a bucket of near boiling water and it stripped her legs of any remaining skin. After she came out of hospital, the district nurse managed to get her to agree, albeit reluctantly, to accept a more conventional treatment."

Horace guffawed. "I'm surprised the mixture didn't explode."

"Indeed," said Marjorie, enjoying the distraction.

"Enough of that," said Edna. "Why was Grace Bloomin'-Jones upset in the first place?

Marjorie had thought her cousin-in-law might have preferred to stay off the subject of Grace Brown-Jones, but her curiosity was getting the better of her.

"Ask Marjorie," said Frederick, leaning back in his chair crossing his arms. "It appears we might have another murder on our plates."

The company at the table went quiet. The corners of Horace's lips turned upward, but Edna gave her daggers.

Chapter 15

Marjorie recounted what had happened earlier, from her early morning walk through the mist covering the shores of Loch Ness – at which point Edna shuddered but said nothing – and on to the culmination of finding Jock McGuire's body. She told how Mick Burns came along and made a futile attempt at resuscitation. Edna scowled when she said that Grace had been speeding through the rain when Mick flagged her down.

"That woman's a headcase, and these two are besotted," she complained.

Horace and Frederick allowed Marjorie to continue her story.

"Grace gave me an exhilarating – take that as terrifying – lift back to the hotel."

Marjorie tucked into the breakfast Brian had brought mid-story with unusual vigour. She had expected discovering a body might have diminished her appetite, but it was the exact opposite. She was eating as if her life depended on it, which it did, she mused. Perhaps it was the fresh Highland air, or the other early morning's exertion having an impact.

Edna harrumphed loudly. "That bloomin' Grace Crackpot-Jones woman turns up everywhere she's not wanted."

"I was pleased to have the lift back. By that time, the rain was coming down in torrents. I might have preferred a less speedy drive, but at least she got me here in one piece."

"More by chance than design, I should think," Edna huffed.

Ignoring Edna, Horace asked.

"What makes you believe the man didn't just slip over? I saw him in the bar last night knocking it back a bit. The spider veins on his face and hands suggest to me he was a heavy drinker. I also noticed him sipping from a flask on the bus after Fred and I found you in the woods yesterday. I thought he'd upset you, so I kept an eye on him for a while."

"You didn't mention any of this to me," said Edna, folding her arms.

"I didn't think it was important and concluded he was a miserable alcoholic who brought an unpleasant atmosphere into the bar and everywhere else he went. I told you already I didn't like him. And while it wouldn't surprise me if someone did want to knock him off, the odds are, it was an accident. It rained hard most of the night. The path must have been lethal."

"But that doesn't account for the forensics van and police cars I saw from my window."

"You must have been eating a tonne of carrots to see that far," said Edna.

"It isn't that far. Besides, I have binoculars."

"And you just happened to be looking out the window," Edna huffed again.

"Back to Horace's observation. You're quite right. It was a little slippery, but the wooden track was well maintained – I almost fell on the shingle – and Jock was wearing sturdy walking boots. The same ones he wore yesterday... I have to say those potato scones were delicious," Marjorie said.

"I'm surprised you can eat anything at all," said Edna. "You realise if there is a killer lurking out there, they might have killed you as well? Not to mention you could have fallen over and broken something. And I bet you weren't carrying your mobile phone. I told you yesterday you shouldn't go wandering off on your own."

Marjorie steepled her hands after laying down her knife and fork in the centre of her plate. "Thankfully, I wasn't murdered, and I didn't fall. I'm still here to tell the tale. Getting back to why I believe Jock McGuire was murdered, and it appears the police agree... it's just that the rock was in the wrong place."

"What are you on about now, Marge? I swear sometimes you're losing your marbles."

"There's nothing wrong with my *marbles,* as you so delicately put it. If you had been listening, I'm merely answering Horace's original question and explaining why I think Jock McGuire's death was homicide."

"You don't think the monster killed him?"

Frederick opened and closed his mouth as if to say something, but decided against it.

"Not unless she popped ashore, hit him over the head with a large boulder and dragged him up to the wooden path, which is over a hundred yards away."

Edna wiped her brow.

"There was blood on a rock next to the poor man's head until the rain washed it away. If he stumbled, he landed violently on his head. Right here." Marjorie rubbed a hand on the left side of her forehead. "It seems all wrong." She didn't mention the feeling she'd had of being watched, not wanting another lecture from Edna about going for unaccompanied strolls or, worse, being accused of imagining things.

"If someone hit him then, we can assume the killer is right-handed," said Horace.

"That narrows it down to ninety per cent of the population," said Edna, scathingly.

"And most likely a hundred per cent of our suspects." Marjorie suggested. "Although we can easily check that out in case any of them are left-handed."

"Even if the death is suspicious, you can't seriously be suggesting you're going to poke your nose in another murder, Marjorie?"

Edna used her full name, which jarred.

"Why don't you just leave these things to the police? I'm sure they can find out who did it. We are in England now, you know."

Horace cleared his throat. "I think you mean Scotland."

Edna's face flushed red, matching today's choice of wig. "You know what I mean. What I'm saying is we don't have to rely on foreign cops bungling their way through an investigation."

"You say some ridiculous things," said Marjorie, irritated. "How do you think foreign cops – as you call them – solve *international crimes,* including murder?"

Intervening before a full-blown argument developed, Frederick said, "Edna has a point about poking our noses in. Perhaps we should let the police get on with their jobs. I can't say I liked Jock McGuire very much and I don't particularly care who killed him, except, of course, I don't condone murder and agree any killer should be caught."

"Pleased to hear it, old chap," said Horace, patting him on the shoulder.

Marjorie had mixed feelings about the whole matter. After all, it had been she who had discovered the body and saw the lifeless eyes staring into the morning sky. It had been she who had witnessed the pool of blood from the man's head and the red-stained rock. And it had been she who had got soaked through doing the right thing.

"What did Grace Brown-Jones have to say about it?" she asked Frederick.

"Not a lot. She was too distressed at first to say anything. Then she told me she had given you a lift back to the hotel after you had found a man dead. She eventually told me who it was that died and said little else on the subject. She laughed when she told me how she startled Mick Burns with a skid stop before he bundled you into her car. Apparently Lamborghinis have great brakes."

"They need to. She drives far too fast," said Marjorie.

"She told me Mick went back to wait for the emergency services while she brought you up here. Apparently you were sodden. I forgot to ask, are you all right?"

"As you see," said Marjorie. "What else did Grace tell you?"

"She said you asked her to call the police and an ambulance and that she'd passed the message on to Nessa although Nessa was in such a state, it was she who ended up calling the ambulance and the police – Brian was statuesque according to her. After putting the phone down, Nessa and Brian had disappeared. I think that's when it sunk in and I came across her; she was pretty shaken up."

"As was I after the brief journey up the drive," said Marjorie, then questioned. "You didn't mention my sleuthing history, did you?"

"*Our* sleuthing history," added Edna, pointedly.

"Yes… our sleuthing history,"

"I almost did. Then I remembered you warned me yesterday not to mention it to anyone else. Hadn't that warning come from Jock?"

Marjorie sipped more tea, enjoying the taste of the now lukewarm liquid. "Indeed, it had. I remember quite clearly what he said. He told me if they found him dead, I might have to use my… erm, our sleuthing skills. He also suggested he thought someone might try to kill him."

Edna examined her polished acrylic nails, pretending to yawn. "I don't suppose he gave you a name? We could have this all wrapped up before the police have time to open a case file."

"Don't be childish," said Marjorie.

Horace shot Edna a gentle warning glance. "Sarcasm doesn't become you, Edna." Turning to Marjorie he said, "Is that why you feel obligated to investigate if it turns out to be, as you say, murder?"

"Now you mention it, I do feel it incumbent upon me, or us…" Marjorie glanced at Edna, "…to at least undertake some background investigating. We could see if the police don't appear to be getting anywhere. The first police officer on the scene was a local, I believe. Depending on his age, he might be biased against McGuire. Everyone else around here seems to have disliked the man. Why not him?"

"Her," said Frederick. "The local bobby is a she, PC Sheila Wood."

"Oh dear, I've just shown unintentional internal bias," said Marjorie. "I was reading an article on the topic recently about how our internal biases cause us to picture men in some jobs and women in others, and how the same stretches to people of colour too. I had formed the image of a white male, aged between thirty and forty, as the local police officer."

"And it turns out she's a white female, aged twenty-eight," said Frederick.

"Erm, Asian female, aged twenty-eight, married to the minister of Scraghead," interrupted Brian, who had appeared to clear the table.

"Oh dear. From now on I will try not to make assumptions, and work hard on quelling any internal bias," said Marjorie. "Do you know anything more, Brian – about what the police are thinking, I mean? Did the officer, PC Wood, know the victim?"

"No, she didn't grow up roond here. The cops are still down there. One of the staff who's just come in said there's a lot of activity and a forensics tent around the scene. I think it'll be a while before they come up here. You go off on your trip. I'm sure they'll still be here when yer get back."

Edna let out a heavy sigh. "I thought they might cancel the loch tour under the circumstances."

"Naw. I've just seen yer leader, Faith, telling Nessa the coach will arrive soon. Here she comes now." Brian took the empty plates and left them to finish their drinks.

"We'll be leaving in fifteen minutes. The bus is collecting guests from the other hotel first, then we'll head off to Inverness to get the boat. I've been told what happened, Marjorie. How are you?"

"I'm fine now I've had an excellent breakfast and plenty of hot tea."

Faith smiled, her eyes gently lighting up.

"Are you sure you're up to going out, Marge? I can stay behind with you if you need to rest after the shock."

"Thank you for your thoughtfulness," said Marjorie. "But right now I'd like to get away from here, and a cruise on the loch is just the thing to take my mind off things."

"There are no vehicles blocking the road," said Faith. "They've driven onto the shingle shore, so we'll have a smooth passage."

"I know Brian said you wouldn't need to stay behind, but don't you have to wait to speak to the police?" Edna tried again.

"No need. I've spoken to Nessa, and she thinks it will be all right for Marjorie to come along. Mick Burns has already given a preliminary statement to Sheila. She's our local police officer."

"So I hear," said Marjorie, casting a triumphant glance towards Edna.

"You don't have to put on a brave face for us, Marge. You've had a nasty shock," said Edna, looking increasingly pale.

"I assure you I'm looking forward to the outing, but you can stay behind if you wish."

"Come on Edna, I'll keep you safe if Nessie pops her head above the water." Horace took the trembling Edna's arm.

Chapter 16

Most of the passengers boarded the chartered boat soon after arriving at the Inverness boatyard. The captain was a man in his fifties with greying hair cut neatly into his neck. He chattered happily while helping them board, assisted by a small crew.

Edna knew she was vacillating, deliberately playing for time to conquer her fear. She dreaded this journey more than anything she had done in years, and she'd done some brave things in her time. The more she told herself her foreboding was irrational, the worse things became. Marge had been patient so far, but she could tell her cousin would only tolerate illogical notions for so long. After what Marge had been through earlier this morning, it was surprising she hadn't already snapped. But that didn't help Edna's anxiety at all.

"My stomach feels a bit off. It must have been something I ate last night," she said to Horace. "Perhaps I'll wait on the bus."

"It's a three- to- four- hour trip, Edna," said Horace, kindly. "You don't want to sit on a rickety old thing for that length of time. The boat's nearly new. I heard the captain telling people as they boarded, it's got a bar and toilets. Get a couple of Scotches inside you and you'll be fine."

"I could go shopping in Inverness." Edna knew she was fooling no-one, and the more she dilly dallied, the more obvious it would become to everyone that her terror was the cause. Pride dictated she should overcome her fears, but the pounding in her heart and the feeling of panic rising in her chest argued otherwise. She was feeling lightheaded.

"If you're well enough to go shopping, you're well enough to come on a boat tour." Horace squeezed her arm reassuringly. "Come on Edna. I promise I'll look after you and I'll not leave you for a minute."

Edna was about to refuse to go when Marge came over. "I've just spoken to Captain Sturgeon."

Edna raised an eyebrow, jaw dropping despite herself.

"I know. I thought the name was too much of a coincidence, so I asked him," Marjorie chuckled. "I don't know what his real name is, but Sturgeon's a nickname. He says he got it because he used to be a fisherman and always netted sturgeon. Anyway, I've spoken to him and he tells me we won't be going anywhere near the places sightings of the Loch Ness Monster have been. Now, come along, Edna. Everyone's waiting for us. If you're struggling with mobility, I can always help you aboard. You can even borrow my stick."

That did it! Edna Parkinton would not be assisted on board any boat by Marjorie Snellthorpe. She would never hear the end of it. "I was just checking I had everything I needed, that's all," she snapped. "It's you who'll need a hand. You'll never manage without your stick. Where is it, by the way?"

Edna caught sight of Marjorie's grin and a twinkle in her bright blue eyes. Ignoring her gloating, she marched towards the vessel and was being thrown into a life jacket before she knew it. Frederick was already ensconced on a bench next to Grace Thingummy-Jones. Edna had got so used to adding her own first part of the double-barrelled name she had forgotten the real version. "Humph! That'll teach Marge Snellthorpe," she muttered.

Marge and Horace arrived by her side once they had donned their life jackets. Following a short safety announcement, the vessel set off along the canal, which was the first part of the tour. After that, they would enter the open waters of the loch. The part she dreaded. The rain had stopped, but Captain Sturgeon informed them there would be a strong westerly wind once they reached

Loch Ness, which told her they were in for a choppy time ahead. No storm could match her feelings, of that she was in no doubt.

"We'll be sheltered for the first hour while travelling along the Caledonian Canal and through a smaller loch. The forecasters tell us the winds will die down pretty soon after entering Loch Ness and you'll find it calmer the further we travel. I'll be pointing out some landmarks along the way and we'll visit a few of the places where our Loch Ness Monster, Nessie, has been spotted in the past. If you see her, let me know and I'll cut the engines." The captain laughed.

Edna's glower at Marge was designed to cut ice, but her cousin smirked annoyingly.

"I must have misheard," she said.

"Whatever, Marge." Edna's annoyance with Marge temporarily helped dispel her fear. Maybe that was her cousin's plan. "Horace. Time for that drink," she snapped. "You coming?" She checked with Marge.

Her self-satisfied cousin shook her head. "I think I'll enjoy the views while we're on the canal."

"Suit yourself." Edna stomped away before pausing at the entrance to the cabin.

Horace took the lead down two wide steps and she followed him into a large interior cabin. Some of the other passengers seemed to have the same idea as them. Large windows offered a sheltered view of the route they were taking. The inside cabin also offered protection and stability, which would be useful when the gale was blowing outside. Horace put his arm out to help her keep balance. No matter how smooth the waters beneath a boat were, there was always a degree of rocking, except, in this instance, they were travelling so slowly she didn't need his help. Still, it was a gracious gesture.

"Warmer in here, isn't it?" he winked. "What are you having?"

"I'll have the Scotch you promised me," she said. Alcoholic courage was what she needed right now.

Edna spied Mick Burns sitting with his daughter and future son-in-law on a long bench lining the cabin in a horseshoe. There were tables and fixed bar stools all around, with plenty of space to accommodate their number. Mick was staring out of a window while the young couple chatted and giggled to each other.

"Why don't you grab us some seats while I get the drinks?" Horace suggested.

Edna was pleased to comply, making her way over to where Mick sat. The young couple shot up, presented with an excuse to escape.

"We're going outside, Dad. You've got company now."

Mick turned around. "What? Oh, hello," he said, giving her a false smile.

Still miffed about last night, she thought. Edna sat next to him, joined moments later by Horace armed with two drinks.

"There. Get that down you."

"Ta," she said, taking a big swig.

Horace leaned forward to speak to Mick. "I hear you had a bit of a shock this morning? Can't have been pleasant."

Horace was stating the obvious again, as was his way, but Edna didn't tell him so this time. The whisky solace was more important right now.

"It was a bit of a rude awakening, but I've seen worse. I was in the fusiliers for a while; did two spells in Iraq, 2004 and 2006. I didn't like it when they combined the regiment, so I didn't reenlist. Turned out I was lucky and got out before they went to Afghanistan. We lost some good men over there."

"I thought you might be ex-military. Something about you," said Horace.

Edna had to stop herself from laughing. Mick Burns was as overweight as she was and looked nothing like a military man in her eyes.

Mick gave Horace a wide grin. "Were you an army man?"

"Only for National Service as a youngster. I did my two years... boy, did I grow up in that time. You had to. I got teased rotten because the other recruits met my mother when she came to see me off… we were heading overseas for military operations in Malaya, as it was called back then."

"Why would your mates be bothered about yer mam seeing you off?" Mick asked.

Edna's ears had pricked up. She didn't know Horace had done National Service, but she knew about his mother, so she guessed what might come next.

"My mother was Romanian. Didn't speak a word of English. There was a lot of prejudice back then, so I had to toughen up fast."

"Sorry to hear that," said Mick.

"It was a lot worse when I got home. Mum had upped and left home; she went back to Romania since the kids had grown up. I read the letter she left to my dad."

That explained Horace's reluctance to go into his parentage when they discovered he spoke fluent Romanian during their last holiday, thought Edna. It was her turn to cheer him up. "Dolly Parton wrote a song about something along those lines. I've covered it on stage in the past. It's called *To Daddy*."

"I've heard the song," said Horace, still sounding doleful. Then he smiled. "I'm still waiting to hear your rendition of *Big Spender*."

"Are you a singer?" Mick asked.

"Was. I haven't been on stage in years." Edna said.

Mick seemed to have got over his mood and unfolded his arms. "By the way. How's your friend, Marjorie? I guess this morning's episode was more shocking for her than for me, finding the body and all."

"She takes that sort of thing in her stride," Edna answered, frowning, still angry with Marge for lying to her about the boat's destination.

Mick was about to respond, but Horace intervened. She had forgotten she wasn't supposed to mention the amateur sleuthing thing.

"I heard the police were down there when we left. What did they have to say about the man's death?" Horace asked.

So much for not getting involved, thought Edna. *He's as bad as Marge.*

"Not a lot. The local bobby took a statement. She wouldn't confirm it was an accident. I got the impression they're not convinced. They could well be right. McGuire was never very popular around these parts. It was a shame he came back at all. He spent the whole day yesterday winding people up about that book of his."

"Did he wind you up?" Edna couldn't resist asking.

"He did, right enough. I never liked him. Even as a kid, he was nothing but trouble. I hadn't laid eyes on him in decades. Then he comes back, shooting his mouth off about things long past. Things that should be forgotten."

"What sort of things?" asked Horace.

"Oh, I don't know; rumours and lies most like. I didn't give him too much of my time, wouldn't give him the satisfaction. He went out with Nessa when they were teenagers – she's the hotel owner."

"Really? I wouldn't have thought he was her type at all," said Edna.

"He was her 'bit of rough', if you know what I mean. Her parents didn't approve, that's all I remember. I liked Nessa myself back then, but she was never interested. I think he bedazzled her; he was streetwise, and she wasn't."

"What happened to them?" Horace asked.

"She came to her senses. I'm pretty sure she split up with him. I reckon he was still carrying a torch for her. Some blokes never let go. Maybe that's why he was so bitter."

"But you said he mentioned things that should be forgotten," Edna pressed. "You were referring to something other than a teenage romance, surely?"

Mick screwed up his eyes as if trying to recall – or maybe forget – something. "I didn't mean anything specific. Anyway, whatever was getting his goat, it's over now. And good riddance."

"I would say it's only just starting," said Horace. "Once the police get involved, they turn over every stone until they uncover everything, relevant or not. If they suspect foul play, they have to, so they can find out who killed him and why."

And if they don't, Marge Snellthorpe certainly will, thought Edna as she scrutinised the straw-coloured liquid in her glass.

Chapter 17

Marjorie felt her bones chill each time the sun went behind a cloud. Their vessel sailed at a meandering pace along the slightly choppy waters of the Caledonian Canal, but she could still feel the occasional gust of wind. Thankfully, she had brought more than one coat with her and this one was thick enough to keep out most of the cold. She wished she'd gone inside with Edna and Horace. A family of four sat on her left and she was on the edge of the bench. The man told her they were staying at the second hotel, but that was the limit of their conversation. The frazzled parents were too busy keeping their two toddlers from wandering off to pay her any attention. Marjorie tried to look at the views beyond the confines of the boat's rails, to no avail. Every time she braved it, her eyes watered from the chilly wind. Giving up, she gazed around the deck. Every so often, her eyes were magnetically drawn to where

Frederick was sitting, engrossed in conversation with Grace Brown-Jones.

Marjorie returned to wondering what Grace had been doing out driving so early in the morning and whether she had been parked on the road near to where she had walked. If so, it put her near where Jock McGuire met his end, and at around the same time. Jock's body had felt cool but not cold to the touch when she leant down before Mick Burns arrived. She noticed he hadn't tried mouth-to-mouth, but neither would she have done. Marjorie recalled hearing Grace's car roar off from close by and not from the hotel itself. Marjorie would have noticed if it had flown past on her meander down from the hotel. Would Grace Brown-Jones be capable of hitting the much taller man hard enough to kill him? It was possible as he was quite spindly, but why would she want to?

As she sat mulling over all the people she had seen or heard Jock McGuire arguing with the day before, she couldn't get away from their conversation in the forest when he appeared to have followed her. *Why on earth did the silly man come back to this area if he believed his life was in danger? And why decide to leave again soon afterwards?* From what Frederick had told them, Jock had been having second thoughts about coming in the first place. Perhaps someone had threatened him. Then there was the mystery person who had put the wind up Jock while he was talking to Frederick. If he hadn't gone for an early morning ramble, he might still be alive. This idea caused her to ponder the decisions people make, and how the simplest choice could end up being the wrong one. It could be as simple as choosing to turn left or right, one of which could turn out to be so costly if they were hit by a bus or attacked by a mugger. *Still, if we knew what was ahead of us, we'd never do anything.* Marjorie exhaled. Whoever killed Jock was intent on finding an opportunity to pounce, unless it was random when the opportunity presented itself. If the killer was determined, though, they would have carried out the grisly deed somewhere else. Jock's walk beside the loch presented the killer with a perfect opening. She wondered whether the person had heard her walking and therefore was less able to make the death look like an accident.

"We're going in for a cup of tea. Would you like to join us?" Frederick's voice jolted Marjorie back to the present.

"Actually, I would. It's getting rather chilly out here."

"Autumn weather can be beautiful in the Highlands, but it's almost always cold. The winds will be bracing across the loch, no matter how much the captain plays them down, so best to get warmed up now," said Grace. "They won't be too strong, though. The forecast is good for most of the day but it'll be cold on the open water. Worth it, though, as the scenery is amazing. There's plenty of shelter on the boat to get good views either way."

"That's reassuring. Thank you." Marjorie stretched as she stood, feeling her bones creak. The bench was cushioned, but not what she'd call comfortable. Frederick held out his arm for her. That was far better than using her stick. Grace sashayed the short distance with elegance and poise, despite the six-inch heels on her bright red designer shoes. Her immaculately tailored white woollen coat was without blemish and worn over tight fitting red trousers. Neither was there a blonde hair protruding from anywhere, and red-framed designer sunglasses matched her shoes. *She obviously uses a good hairspray,* thought Marjorie, imagining the blonde woman in a hairspray advert with the headline: Never a hair out of place. She giggled.

Frederick raised a quizzical eyebrow while assisting her down the steps into the inner cabin. Their eyes locked onto each other's for a moment and time appeared to stand still, but not for long enough.

"Over here, Marge." Edna's loud voice crashed through the stillness, breaking the spell.

"I'll pay," said Marjorie to Frederick after giving Edna a wave. Edna's grin turned to a frown when she realised Grace Brown-Jones was with them.

"But—" Fred tried.

"No. I insist. I can't have you and Horace paying all the time. Tea for three?" Marjorie checked with Grace, who nodded.

"Thank you."

After ordering a pot of tea for three, the crewman encouraged them to sit down. "I'll bring it over," he said.

There were fixed tables in front of a long bench. Edna cleared enough space for Marjorie to take a seat before huffing and puffing at a group of young people sat on bar stools in front of them. The youngsters ended up shrugging their shoulders and moving away from the madwoman with the fiery red hair. *Who can blame them?* Thought Marjorie. Grace and Frederick took the stools, the former managing to perch elegantly. She was the type of woman who would look gorgeous wearing a bin bag, just like her dear friend Rachel. The only difference was Grace was much older than her young friend.

The crewman brought a tray with three mugs of tea and plonked it on the table. He left sachets of sugar for them to help themselves to and a jug of milk. "Not quite what I ordered," said Marjorie to Frederick.

"Don't tell me you were expecting tea in a china teapot with cups and saucers?" Edna clearly hadn't forgiven her for the subterfuge at the marina. It had been a well-intentioned ploy, even if her cousin-in-law didn't see it that way.

"These are my other travelling companions," Frederick said to Grace. "Edna Parkinton and Horace Tyler." Marjorie noticed he omitted the word, friends.

"Pleased to meet you," said Grace in her beautiful Scottish accent.

"Charmed," said Horace, holding out his hand, almost drooling. Edna's curt nod was ignored.

Grace took Horace's hand and shook it firmly. "Have you been to the Highlands before?"

From that moment, Horace commandeered Grace's attention with tales of his travels, much to Edna's disgust. Marjorie could sense Edna's hackles rising, so she nudged her.

"How are you feeling?" she asked, lowering her voice.

"Much better now I've had a couple of these." Edna took an inelegant swig from her glass. "Is it my imagination, or is the boat slowing down?"

"There's a speed limit on the canal. He might be stuck behind a slower vessel," said Frederick, taking a drink from his mug. He too eyed Horace warily, clearly wanting to be the focus of Grace's attention once more, but the blonde woman was enthralled with Horace's stories.

Turning her back to Horace, Edna said. "We spoke to Mick Burns when we got here. He said the police are treating that death as suspicious. Seems you're right again, Marge."

"It didn't take a rocket scientist to work that one out," Marjorie countered. "Let's hope they find who is responsible quickly." Marjorie had been observing Grace and noticed a slight flicker of interest, although she was pretending not to be listening.

"He said something about Jock McGuire stirring things up. Stuff from the past that should be left alone, but when we asked him what he meant by that, he clammed up good and proper. Couldn't wait to get out of here."

"I see," said Marjorie. "Mind you. Wasn't that Jock's intention in writing his book? Dredging up history."

"An Exposé, he called it," added Frederick.

"Yeah it was. But I thought you told us he was leaving today?" Edna said accusingly, as if Frederick could have done something about Jock McGuire's demise.

"Poor chap didn't get the chance, did he?" Frederick said, taking another sip of the hot tea.

"Mick also told us Jock and Nessa used to be an item." Edna raised both eyebrows. "Imagine those two together. According to him, Jock was her bit of rough. I think he was jealous because he admitted fancying her himself back in the day."

"That might account for Nessa's reaction yesterday," said Marjorie. "I can't say I'm surprised, though. They are, or rather were, of a similar age. It can't have been easy for teenagers growing up in such a tightly knit community, with everybody knowing everybody else. I wonder whether Nessa ever married."

Horace and Grace had stopped speaking and were now openly listening.

"Nessa married not long after she split with Phil McGuire – the name we knew him by," said Grace. "The marriage didn't work out."

"Does her ex still live in the area?" Marjorie asked.

"No. They moved to Edinburgh, but she came back after the divorce. I thought there was a child, but she doesn't talk about it, and I don't pry."

Interesting, thought Marjorie.

"When Nessa's dad died, she inherited his money; sold the family home and bought the land for the hotel off of us. We felt it would be better put to good use than left for grazing. She's done well for herself. I'm almost sorry we didn't think of doing something like that ourselves. I hope this death business doesn't put a dampener on her ambitions for the place."

"Do you own a lot of the land around here?" Horace asked.

"A fair bit. I run the land side of our estate and my husband runs stables. He loves racehorses. He's south of the border at the moment, selling, buying, or both. I ride, but horse racing doesn't interest me."

Horace nodded his head, clearly impressed, or beguiled and unashamedly pleased Grace's husband was out of the country.

Before Edna could embarrass him with a caustic remark, Marjorie changed the subject.

"Is the waiter, Brian, also from around here?" Marjorie felt the relationship between the surly man and the hotel owner was close, almost like father and daughter.

"Brian Cahill you mean? Yes, he was Nessa's dad's business partner – employee really – Nessa's dad told people he was a partner to big him up. They were like brothers. Nessa promised her dad she'd look after him when he was gone. Brian's wife died a few years back, and he was left in debt after paying for a private nurse to care for her. In turn, he looks out for Nessa, treats her like the daughter he never had. And she looks out for him by giving him work and wages. That way, he keeps his self-respect. It works for both of them."

"Sounds like an excellent arrangement. It's good to know there's still some kindness in the world," said Marjorie. "Brian didn't appear to like Jock-AKA-Phil."

"Nobody liked Phil McGuire. He took Nessa in for a while, but he was bad news. Having come across him yesterday, he hadn't changed a bit. As the saying goes: a leopard never changes its spots."

Edna took the opening with all the lack of subtlety she was prone to. "Weren't you driving around early this morning near to where Jock McGuire died?" Her accusation hit Grace with its full force.

Grace's mouth twitched.

Thank you, Edna. We'll get nothing more out of her now, thought Marjorie.

Chapter 18

An announcement from Captain Sturgeon interrupted the awkward moment between Grace and Edna.

"Ladies and gentlemen, we're just making our approach alongside Aldourie Castle. If you move over to the port side, that's the left for you landlubbers, you'll get a fine view of the castle and its grounds. I'll slow right down so you can take some photos before we head on to Loch Ness. Aldourie Castle's the only habitable castle on the shores of the loch. If you like the look of it, they take private bookings should you fancy hiring a castle for a wee stay."

Grace took her opportunity, politely excusing herself during the captain's announcement.

"Staying in a castle, eh? Right up your street, Marge," said Edna.

Marjorie ignored the dig. "I would have been more interested in eliciting further information about our list of suspects from Grace had you not frightened her off."

"Me too," said Frederick.

"And I would have liked to talk to the lady some more. She's an interesting woman," said Horace. "Has a wealth of knowledge about the area, land management and all sorts of things."

"Not to mention the good looks and the Lamborghini," Edna retorted, arms folded. "You're so gullible. It's not genuine, you know, all that enthusiasm for your stories. Besides, I didn't drive her away, and if I did, she shouldn't be so precious."

"You all but accused her of being a killer," interjected Frederick.

"I did not! Still, there's no doubt she's a suspect on Marge's list. And as my dear cousin is intent on playing detective again, I thought I'd help her get on with it. No point pussyfooting around. All I did was ask what she was doing out so early near the scene of the crime – if it was a crime. I don't see why she should take offence unless she's got something to hide."

"For your information," Frederick said. "Grace was out early checking on a red deer stag that's been highly successful in ruts over the past few seasons. He has quite a harem to protect. That's what she was doing out so early. Apparently, the rut starts a few hours after dawn and a few hours before dusk. She wanted to check on his condition before coming on the boat trip."

"Why didn't she just say so?" queried Marjorie.

"I expect the poor woman didn't like our Edna's tone," said Horace, stroking his chin. "You have a way with words." He looked at Edna.

"Humph. I don't know why you're all ganging up on me. I only asked what Marge was wondering." Edna pouted.

"It's not what you say. It's how you put it," said Marjorie. "Never mind that now. Let's take a glance at this castle the captain's been raving about before we move onto the open water."

"Good idea," said Horace.

Marjorie suspected the sparkle in his eyes and the jaunt in his step as he leapt up and sauntered outside had more to do with Grace Brown-Jones than a Scottish castle.

"I'll stay here so we don't lose the seats. It'll be far too cold out there once we arrive at Loch Ness and I wouldn't want Marjorie to catch a chill."

It was another of the few occasions when Edna used her proper name, which Marjorie should have been pleased about, except it didn't sound right coming from her cousin-in-law's mouth. That, and the fact it was dripping with sarcasm in order to hide her real reason for staying inside, caused it to jar. "Thank you for your concern," she said, not wishing to retaliate by drawing any further attention to Edna's fear of a monster in the depths beneath.

"Shall we get on, then?" Frederick had waited for her.

Once on deck, the winds were blowing in from the west and Marjorie felt the chill on her face. "I suppose we should be thankful the wind's not coming from the east."

Frederick didn't hear her above the chatter of people gathering on the port side of the boat. If Horace had been hoping for another tête-à-tête with Grace, he was to be disappointed. She was in earnest conversation with Mick Burns. It was no surprise that they knew each other; it seemed most people who had grown up in the area were acquainted even if they had since gone their separate ways. Mick's daughter must have left him to his own devices again, poor man. Marjorie couldn't help feeling sorry for the widower, trying to spirit up happier memories that were clearly eluding him. She was certain he wouldn't have come if he'd known Jock, AKA Phil McGuire, would be on the trip. A thought struck her as she watched. What if Jock had told them all he was coming to wind them up? What if his targets were here by design? If so, no-one had thought to mention it to Nessa. Marjorie was certain her shocked reaction the day before had been genuine. While Frederick listened to passengers talking about Aldourie Castle and its history, Marjorie kept her eyes fixed on Mick and Grace. He too was out early this morning and close to where she found the body. He hadn't seemed too surprised at finding the body, jumping straight into resuscitation. Was that instinct or the covering behaviour of a killer?

"I can tell your brain's still ticking over, Marjorie. Shall we go back inside? The wind's getting up a bit."

Horace must have decided not to pursue Grace while she was otherwise engaged. She sensed Frederick hadn't given up. Marjorie noticed his surreptitious glances over to where the attractive woman remained in conversation with Mick Burns.

"Good idea. We ought to keep Edna company anyway. I didn't realise she took this monster thing so seriously. I've never seen her so spooked."

"She'll be all right once today's trip is over. It's brave of her to come at all when she's so frightened. I admire that."

"You're quite right," said Marjorie. "Too many people allow their fears to overwhelm them; Edna's not one to do that. We should try to keep her distracted and help her through the next few hours."

They needn't have worried. By the time they reached Edna, the woman was sat, head back, mouth wide open, snoring loudly with a half-empty glass in front of her. The red wig had slipped back, revealing stubble at the hairline.

"I say," said Horace. "It looks like she might have had one Scotch too many."

There was a lot of noise inside the cabin. Marjorie marvelled at her cousin-in-law being able to sleep through the racket. "Do you think she's all right?"

Horace sat next to Edna, nudging her gently, but got no response. Marjorie tried from the other side, grabbing her shoulder. "Edna?"

"Is everything okay?" The crewman from behind the bar appeared.

"How many more whiskies did she have after we left?" Horace asked.

"None, as far as I know. The lady hasn't been to the bar at all. But someone else could have bought her one. Our Scotch is popular."

Marjorie picked up Edna's glass, scrutinising it, and noticed a sediment of white powder lining the bottom. She showed it to Horace.

"Not to worry," said Horace to the crewman. "She must have been feeling seasick and taken some pills."

The crewman arched an eyebrow, but appeared relieved at the same time. "I'd hate to see what she'd be like if the water was rough," he muttered, and left them to it.

"Is that what you really think?" asked Marjorie, feeling Edna's wrist for a pulse. It was slow, but strong. Edna's snoring sounded like a trombone.

Horace placed a hand under her chin and the other on her forehead as her head fell forwards. He gently placed it so that her neck was stretched and her airway clear. It helped quieten the snoring. "It makes sense to me. She might have taken a sleeping pill or a sedative. I know she has some. She mentioned it once."

"Not so brave after all," said Marjorie. "Unless someone else sedated her."

"Who would do that? And why?" quizzed Horace.

"I'm not certain. She's upset two people that we know of. Goodness knows how many others she might have annoyed. I think she mentioned Mick Burns going off in a huff and we saw how Grace reacted to her veiled – or not so veiled – accusation."

"She was just being Edna. You know how she is; a little blunt, but nothing to warrant anyone drugging her. Besides, Mick and Grace were both outside the whole time we were."

"Hmm," said Marjorie, rubbing her temple. "Perhaps she couldn't face a meeting with Nessie."

Horace chortled. "I'm sure that's it. As I said, I didn't see Grace or Mick move, and I can't imagine why either of them would want to slip her a mickey. Although, I must admit, I didn't see them the whole time. I was chatting to Faith and young Daisy for a while."

"No. You're quite right. They didn't leave the deck."

"I also ran into Brian Cahill on deck," said Horace

"Brian from the hotel? What's he doing here?"

"Acting as first mate for the captain. Apparently, the other guy took ill at the last minute, so Sturgeon phoned the hotel and asked if Brian could step in. He told me there were only a couple of guests left at the hotel, so Nessa let him come. He's born and bred around here and knows his way around boats. To be honest, it's the happiest I've seen him since we arrived, the first time the man's passed the time of day with me. Maybe he doesn't enjoy being a waiter-cum-babysitter after all."

"Interesting. I wonder if he knows his way around sedatives," said Marjorie.

"Brian would have no reason to drug Edna. Besides, I think she's the one of us he's warmed to; present company excepted of course. The most likely explanation is, as you suggested, her anxiety got the better of her and she took a tablet. She'd knocked back quite a few whiskies as well."

"Nevertheless, you should ask her not to be so outspoken in the future. There's no point in me trying to say anything. She wouldn't listen."

"I can try but—"

"Edna is Edna. I understand."

Horace was most probably right about Edna's anxiety getting the better of her, but after this morning's find, Marjorie wasn't happy with anything that seemed out of the ordinary.

"What happened to her?" Frederick plonked himself down on a barstool, bringing her wonderings to an end.

"A bit too much Scotch," explained Horace. "I take it you didn't get anywhere either?" he smirked.

Frederick ignored his reference to their fondness for a certain woman. Marjorie shook her head. *Why do men see everything as a competition?* Frederick didn't question the explanation of Edna sleeping in the rowdy cabin.

Marjorie showed him the glass. "It appears she might have taken a tablet of some sort. I don't suppose you would know what that is with your background in chemistry?"

"Not without sending it off to a lab or taking a blood sample from Edna. It's a white sediment, and looking at her, I'd say she took a sleeping pill or a Valium." Frederick sounded moody, and his tone lacked empathy.

The Grace Brown-Jones effect, Marjorie concluded.

Edna let out an excessively loud snore, which seemed to jolt her eyes open, but then she closed them again. "It's a good job people are too busy nattering to notice her," said Horace.

"Or too indifferent. People don't care in the same way they used to," said Frederick.

"Perhaps they don't," said Marjorie, still not convinced her cousin-in-law had willingly taken a sleeping tablet, but she couldn't explain why she felt otherwise.

At that moment, she caught sight of someone else watching them from the other side of the cabin.

Chapter 19

Marjorie wracked her brains before recognising the young woman as Terry Stewart, the head gardener's wife. She thought some more, trying to recall her name, uncertain whether Terry had mentioned it when she spoke with him the day before. The woman's eyelids dropped when she realised she had been spotted.

"Over there." Marjorie inclined her head in Mrs Stewart's direction, who was now pretending to read a magazine.

"What?" Horace asked.

Lowering her voice, Marjorie whispered, "It's the head gardener's wife. She was on the coach yesterday with her husband. I saw them having a heated argument with Jock when we were watching salmon."

"And I thought you were interested in the salmon." Frederick feigned hurt.

"I was," Marjorie smiled, "but when you pointed McGuire out to me, he was arguing with a couple. Didn't you notice?"

"I did, as a matter of fact. Terry and Gemma. Mick introduced me to them when we got back to the carpark before we came looking for you. Everyone knows everyone who grew up around here."

"Terry didn't grow up here. He's from Yorkshire, but his wife did. I met him in the grounds yesterday afternoon; a friendly man until the point when I mentioned Jock and the argument. His demeanour changed completely. I'm afraid the mere mention of that man's name left a bitter taste in everyone's mouth."

"It's not like you to upset people, Marjorie. That's Edna's job," said Horace.

"What is?" Edna had finally awoken from her slumber.

"Nothing. What happened to you? You were out for the count," Horace quizzed.

"Too much Scotch, I suspect."

"So what's this?" Marjorie pointed to the remnants in the glass.

"What? Oh that. I was getting heartburn, so I took a couple of Alka-Seltzer."

"Ah," Frederick pursed his lips, "the magic sodium bicarbonate. That explains it."

Marjorie huffed, "Mixed in a glass of whisky? Edna Parkinton, you really are unbelievable at times."

"I didn't want us to lose our seats; it was getting busy in here. Besides, it tasted better with Scotch than it does in water. Explains what?" Edna's eyes narrowed.

Marjorie opened her mouth to speak, but closed it again. There was no point in pursuing this conversation any further. Deep down, she felt relief that Edna hadn't been drugged and also that she hadn't mixed alcohol and sedation, which could be dangerous.

"We thought you might have taken a sedative," explained Horace.

"So, is the trip over?" Edna's eyes sparkled.

Horace grinned. "Not at all. You haven't missed much; we're just arriving at Loch Ness now."

"Great," Edna groaned.

The rest of the tour of Loch Ness passed without mishap. The captain pointed out the most famous landmarks as they sailed, stopping at various intervals to allow passengers to take photographs.

Gemma Stewart remained in the same place throughout, either stealthily watching them while pretend-reading her magazine or casting her eyes on the loch. Marjorie was convinced that she was more interested in them than the sights, as every so often their eyes met before the other woman broke eye contact. What she couldn't work out was why she should interest her unless her husband Terry had said something about their conversation in the grounds yesterday. If her presence and continual staring were meant to intimidate her, it was having the opposite effect. Gemma Stewart had become a person of interest, and Marjorie had every intention of finding out what power Jock had wielded over her and whether it was enough to provoke her to kill him.

***

The coach came to a standstill, unable to turn into Nessie's Lochside Hotel because of a marked police van blocking the entrance. The guests staying at Nessie's groaned. People from the second hotel were rubbernecking through the window.

"I wonder what that's all about?" A diminutive man said to his wife.

Marjorie nudged Edna. "Don't say anything. Let people enjoy their holiday."

"What makes you think I was going to tell them?" Edna hissed.

"Something about the way you opened your mouth."

Daisy's voice burst through the intercom. "It appears there's a problem near the shore…"

"Understatement," whispered Marjorie.

"…We'll drive on to our hotel first, folks. The bus will come back to Nessie's afterwards," Daisy finished.

Marjorie jumped up from her seat and scurried down to the front of the coach. "Hold on a minute! Let me out here. I'll find someone to move that thing out of the way for when you get back."

Faith grinned, eyes shining. "Go ahead," she said to the driver, who opened the doors.

Marjorie climbed down and Faith got off for a moment. "I know what you're up to, Marjorie. Just be careful."

"I do not know what you mean," Marjorie chuckled.

"We'll come too. We don't want 'er falling over." Edna almost tumbled over in her rush to get off the coach, but Horace caught her from behind. Frederick appeared after them.

"The awesome foursome," Faith laughed as she got back on the bus, shaking her head. "See you soon."

"Right team," said Horace. "What's the plan?"

"Yeah, Marge. We know you weren't just going to ask someone to move that van." Edna's speech was still slurred from the alcohol.

"Was it that obvious?"

"Not to anyone else, but it was to us," said Frederick.

"I think Mick Burns might have guessed," said Horace. "He gave me an odd stare when I passed him."

"What about the bleached blonde?" Edna clearly couldn't resist the dig.

"Oh, I doubt she would have given it any thought," said Frederick. "Although if you're looking for information, Marjorie, I don't think you're going to get very far. Look."

Frederick was right. Blue and white police tape created a closed section, cordoning off the area across the road. "Hmm. I wonder if I should go underneath and ask them to move their vehicle. I could also say I wanted to mention something about finding the body this morning. It was me who discovered the dead man, after all."

"Then we'll say we're supporting you because you've been so upset by it all," suggested Horace, who had already crossed the road and was standing, holding up the tape with his right hand.

"Erm, I don't like to dampen your spirits, but I think it says POLICE LINE DO NOT CROSS for a reason," said Edna.

"Nonsense. We're tourists. They have no business closing the path to the shore anyway. It doesn't send out the right message to people visiting the area," said Marjorie, jutting out her chin before stooping down to get underneath the tape.

"I don't think we should all go," said Frederick.

"Well, I'm happy to stay behind," said Edna. "I've had enough stress for one day without spending the night in a police cell."

Marjorie strode away, leaving Edna and Frederick on the right side of the cordon. Horace, though, was hot on her heels. "She's had too much of something, that's for sure, but it can hardly be called stress. The woman slept most of the day."

"I think she did remarkably, considering she still believes the monster killed our Jock McGuire," Horace countered.

"Pah. Stuff and nonsense. The only monster involved in this case comes in human form."

"What are we going to say to these chaps?" Horace asked.

"We'll start by asking them to move their van from blocking the entrance and, if we get the opportunity, I'll let them know it was me who found the body. It depends how friendly they are."

"Judging by the bloke heading our way, not so much."

Horace was right. The plain-clothes officer heading towards them was waving his arms about as if trying to shoo chickens back into a coop. He was also yelling… they weren't close enough to hear what he was saying, but his intent was clear. He wanted them out of there.

Marjorie continued walking towards the red-faced man.

Horace hesitated. "I think we should probably head back."

"OY! Can't you read? Turn around and get back the way you came. You cannae come doon here."

Marjorie stopped, waiting for the man she assumed was a police officer to come within talking, rather than shouting, range. He was still shouting, as if by bellowing he could make up for the distance. As he got closer, his purple face suggested, as well as being angry, he might not be used to exercise.

"I'm not sure if you're aware, officer, but there's a police van blocking the entrance to our hotel. The coach driver couldn't get through and will be back soon. Would you mind asking someone to move it?"

The man turned around, barking his orders. "FRANK! GET UP HERE WILL YER?"

A leaner plain-clothed officer poked his head out from behind the forensics tent. He removed a pair of gloves, stuffed them in his pocket and headed towards them.

"Is Frank the driver?" Horace raised an eyebrow.

"Officer Charles to you," said the beefy man. "Frank to us."

"Hi," a younger detective with black hair tied in a ponytail joined them. "What is it?"

"Escort these people away from my crime scene, and when you're done, move yer van. Apparently it's blocking the entrance to Nessie's."

"Right. Sorry, Sarge. I should've known." His words hung in the wind as the sergeant abruptly turned about and stomped back towards the forensics tent.

"Is he always so welcoming?" Horace asked.

"Oh no. He's usually much worse. You caught him on a good day." Officer Charles grinned. "Here, you'd better put these overshoes on. I'm DC Frankie Charles. Frank's my real name; only the sarge uses it."

Marjorie rolled her eyes. "I know that feeling in reverse. I'm Marjorie, Marjorie Snellthorpe, and this is Horace Tyler."

"Okay, Mrs Snellthorpe, Mr Tyler, follow me. Sergeant Bell's not known for his tolerance, so we'd better not hang aboot."

"Please call me Horace." Horace's eyes brightened as he gazed at Frank Charles's back, which was covered in white chalk.

"Focus, Horace," said Marjorie.

"What do you think I'm doing?" He giggled.

Frankie swivelled his head back. Eyebrows raised. "Are you the Mrs Snellthorpe who found the body?"

"Indeed I am."

They had reached the cordon, and Frankie lifted the tape to allow them through. Frederick and Edna were nowhere to be seen.

"In that case, I'll give youse a lift back to the hotel and take a statement from Mrs Snellthorpe, if yer don't mind?"

"That would be just perfect," said Marjorie, winking at Horace. "I've never travelled in a police van before."

"Well hop in, I'll show you how she works."

Marjorie refrained from saying her hopping days were long gone and was grateful when Horace assisted her climb into the van.

Once inside, Frankie showed them the controls, pointing to a control panel on the dashboard. "From here we can switch on the blue lights, sound the siren, turn the light on in the cell."

"The cell?" asked Marjorie.

"Aye. The detention cell in the back when we have prisoners."

"Of course," she said.

"There's an extraction fan if they need air back there. That button there tells control we're at the scene. I don't get to drive a van so much these days, but my car's in the garage and we were short on vehicles."

Marjorie felt the van's controls were pretty much self-explanatory, but there was no harm behaving as if they were not. Once Frankie pulled the van up outside of the hotel, she felt she had the measure of the amiable young detective. He liked to talk and was open, unlike his sergeant.

"How long have you been in the force?" Horace asked.

"About five years. My dad told me to go into business, so I did the opposite." He threw his head back, laughing.

Chapter 20

"I'm not waiting here while Marge goes off on one of her fishing trips. She'll get us all in trouble." Edna was put out that Horace had chosen to go off with her cousin instead of staying with her.

"You're the one who was in such a hurry to get off the coach in the first place," said Fred, pulling his hat further down to shield his head from the chilly wind blowing in from the loch.

"I didn't want her going off and getting herself killed, that's all. She's not so steady on her feet these days and flat-out refuses to use her stick most of the time." Edna didn't tell Fred, but being close to the loch again at dusk was giving her goose pimples. She didn't feel as safe without Horace. "Anyway, there's not much we can do waiting here in the cold; I'm going to walk up to the hotel. You coming or not?"

Fred shifted his eyes from where Marge and Horace had gone before pulling his coat closer to his body. "There is an icy nip in the air. We can order hot drinks for when they get back."

Edna found the walk up the track difficult, pausing to catch her breath about three times, and by the time they reached the steps, she was huffing and puffing like a steam engine. She stopped again. "That hill's harder than it looks."

Fred wasn't even out of breath, but he was sensitive enough not to mention it. "These gradual inclines can take you by surprise. I say, are you all right? You've gone very pale."

"I'm fine. Too much alcohol and not enough food this afternoon. A nice hot chocolate should do the trick."

"Come on then, let's get you inside." Fred held his arm out for her.

Edna had to stop herself giggling at the smaller man, thinking for one moment he could support her much larger frame were she to topple over. She ignored the offer and found the energy to climb the steps into the hotel lobby. "At least there's one positive. That wretched Grace Precious-Jones isn't here."

Fred looked miffed at her slighting his new fancy woman. "I'm rather pleased the foreboding Brian isn't here," he said. "I wonder where he got to?"

"Maybe drove back by himself. I bet he knows another way into the hotel. He's okay when you get to know him; he's one of those who's got a heart of gold underneath the rough exterior."

"I'll take your word for it," said Fred.

They took a seat in the lobby and were approached by a young waitress Edna hadn't seen before after Fred gave her a nod.

"What can I get yer?"

"Hot chocolate," said Edna.

"I'll have a coffee please," said Fred. "Do you think we should order a pot of tea for Marjorie?"

Edna shrugged. Sometimes Marge's good fortune and determination to investigate dead bodies annoyed her, and this was one of those times. Why was it everyone followed where her cousin led? It was beyond her. "Up to you…"

Fred turned to the waitress. "A pot of tea, please. What do you think Horace would like?" he turned to Edna again.

"How should I know? I'm not his keeper."

"That will be all for now," said Fred.

The waitress seemed pleased to get away. Edna wished she could control her anger, but there were occasions when she couldn't help herself. If Fred had gone with Marge and Horace had stayed with her, she would have felt less betrayed. She knew she was being stupid and in all honesty recognised that Horace was far more adventurous than Fred, so it was bound to be him throwing caution to the wind, but it still got to her. What with that and Grace Flippin'-Jones ruining their holiday, she was beginning to wish she had never come. She and Fred sat in silence until the drinks came.

The hot chocolate soothed her and the sugar and caffeine kick soon made her feel better. "Do you think that

Jock bloke was topped?" she asked Fred, who was browsing through a complimentary newspaper.

"Sorry?"

"I asked if you agreed with Marge that the Jock fella was murdered?"

"It seems the police do from what we've heard and seen so far, and I trust Marjorie's judgement. She was right in Romania, wasn't she?"

"It wasn't all her. We helped as well," snapped Edna.

"Jock seemed to have a lot of enemies up here; it makes you wonder why he came back at all. Why didn't he just write his book and publish it from a distance?"

"That's easy. Men like him like controlling the narrative, as Marge would say. He was malicious, wanted to let his old pals know what he was up to – put the wind up them, you know?"

Fred folded the newspaper he had picked up when Edna was ignoring him and returned it to the table. Rubbing his bald head, having finally removed the hat, he said. "It's almost as if he had a death wish. I'd like to get hold of that manuscript. I suppose he had it with him."

"Good idea. We should search his room; that's what Marge would do."

Fred's eyes bulged. "Won't the police have done that already? Besides, I wouldn't feel any more comfortable mooching around in a dead man's room than I would have done crossing a police cordon."

"Better we do it than the police. I don't expect they've done much searching yet. They're hardly overflowing with numbers up here, are they? I say we go and take a look." She didn't want to say she wanted to be one step ahead of Marge for a change, otherwise Fred wouldn't go along with her plan.

Fred rubbed the back of his head, shaking it at the same time. "I don't know. Besides, we don't have a key."

"In case you haven't noticed, there's no-one manning reception. That waitress seems to be doing everything, and she's nattering in the kitchen. Do you know what room he was in?"

"Thirty-five. I asked at reception yesterday when I wanted to catch a word with him, just in case I had to go to his room."

"Right. Time for action." Before Fred had a chance to say anything, Edna had jumped up, leaned over the reception desk and grabbed the key for number thirty-five. Her room was forty-five, so she could always say she had taken it by mistake if anyone challenged them.

The waitress returned to the lobby just as they were making for the stairs.

"Don't you want this tea?" she called.

"If you see a little woman with snow-white hair come in with a tall bloke wearing a toupee, it's for her." Edna chuckled as she grabbed Fred's hand, pulling him up the stairs before he could change his mind.

***

As soon as they were inside Jock McGuire's room with the door closed behind them, Edna switched on the light.

"Goodness me!" exclaimed Fred.

"You've got that right." Edna trembled slightly as they surveyed the chaotic scene in front of them. "Someone else got here first."

"I think we should go," said Fred, wiping sweat from his brow.

"Not yet," Edna's determination returned as she scanned the room, thinking. *What would Marjorie do?* "Let's look around. Maybe whoever did this missed something."

Fred stood at the door, ready to run, but Edna made her way to the pile of clothes strewn around the suitcase. She rifled through what the intruder had left of Jock McGuire's belongings.

"Shouldn't you be wearing gloves or something?" said Fred.

Edna puffed out a burst of air. "Like I carry them around in my handbag. Don't just stand there; take a look in the drawers, he might have left a clue."

Fred obeyed and headed to the chest next to the enormous wardrobe. "At least we know he intended to leave this morning," he said.

"Yeah. Shame he decided to go for a morning stroll. He might have been back under the rock he crawled out of by now instead of on a slab." Edna's fingers perused the dead man's belongings, picking each item up, checking trouser and jacket pockets, then putting them back in as close a position as she found them that she could remember.

After what Edna would call a cursory look through drawers, Fred said. "There's nothing here. Let's go."

"Wait. Check under the mattress. In films, people always hide stuff under the mattress."

Fred sighed heavily, but did as she asked. "He was packed, ready to leave. There won't be anything."

As it turned out, Fred was right. There was nothing under the pillows or the mattress or the bed.

"Come on, brain. Think," Edna chastised herself.

"Can we go now?"

Fred's whining was getting on her nerves as well as the frustration at not having found anything. Edna was sitting on the edge of the bed, staring at the suitcase. "I suppose so."

"Hang on! There's another place people hide things in films," said Fred, grabbing the case. "Check the lining."

Edna ran her hands along the bottom of the case and felt a ridge. Running her fingers along the edges, she eventually came to a tab, which she pulled. The case's false bottom revealed a startling find.

Fred's mouth dropped open.

"See. I told you we'd find something," Edna's voice squeaked in triumph.

Chapter 21

Edna and Frederick were not in the lobby when Marjorie, Horace, and Frankie entered the hotel.

"Where are the others? Trust Edna to go off in a huff." No doubt Edna was still reeling over Grace Brown-Jones attracting Horace's attention. *Either that, or she's got a headache after the stress and the amount of alcohol she consumed.*

Horace shrugged.

Marjorie didn't have time to say anything else to Horace because she had to dodge a frantic Nessa rushing towards them or be knocked over.

"Frankie Charles! It's been too long." Nessa looked the young policeman up and down before throwing her arms around him.

Frankie's cheeks shone from blushing as he disentangled himself from the proprietor's embrace. He gathered himself together and straightened his shoulders. "I don't have time to talk. I'm working."

Nessa backed off, holding her right cheek as if someone had slapped her. "Sorry, I'm so sorry."

Marjorie and Horace watched on in confusion as Nessa scooted away as fast as she had come.

Horace's eyes widened, but he didn't say anything.

Frankie cleared his throat, breaking the silence. It was clear to Marjorie he was embarrassed. He removed a notebook from his pocket and turned to Marjorie. "Mrs Snellthorpe. Do you mind if I take that statement now?"

"I'll go and change, then see if I can find the others. We'll wait for you in the bar," said Horace.

Marjorie nodded. "Good idea. I don't think I'll be too long. There's not too much to say."

The transformation in Frankie's behaviour and demeanour were remarkable and puzzling. Marjorie followed him into a private room off the back of reception. How did he know it was there? The police must have commandeered the room for interviews while they were out, but it was clear from Nessa's warm greeting and Frankie's frosty reception she hadn't seen him before that moment.

After Frankie closed the door, Marjorie asked. "Did you grow up near here?"

The officer smiled, but this time it didn't reach his eyes. "No, I grew up in Edinburgh, but I've pounded the beat in Inverness and trudged around all the villages at one time or another. They mainly stationed me in Inverness. Now I've joined the detective team, I go wherever there's a need. I'm working towards my sergeant's exams."

The tension in his jaw relaxed a little.

"This is such a beautiful part of the world. I don't suppose you get many murders outside of the big cities. I'm assuming you think it was murder."

"Aye. We see a few, but I've never been to one around here. Still, I'm fairly new to the team."

"Who's in charge of the investigation?" Marjorie quizzed.

"DI Patricia Bloom. She's from the south of the border, like you. I've been seconded to her team because she's one of the most experienced serious crime officers and she's got a DS vacancy. If I pass my sergeant's, I'll be up for filling that vacancy. We're short of boots on the ground, if you know what I mean."

"I do. I take it your current title, DC, means detective constable?" Marjorie knew full well what it meant, but she wanted him to think her an ignorant old woman rather than an interested sleuth.

"Aye, although it's not always as exciting as it sounds, being a detective. There's a lot of legwork in it. The DI's a good sort, although she can be a bit scatty according to the sarge."

Marjorie suspected Sergeant Bell might have issues with a female boss judging by his manner, so his opinion wouldn't hold too much sway with her. Time to ask the burning question before they got down to the formal interview. "Did you know the dead man, Frankie?"

Frankie was holding out a chair for her and looked down through perceptive green eyes. "What makes you ask that?"

"It appears everyone else around here did; I just wondered if your paths had crossed at all?"

Having secured Marjorie in her seat, Frankie pulled a chair up so they were sitting side-on. He laid his notebook on the desk and she noticed he not only chewed his fingernails to the quick but also the tip of his pen. "I'm told he left the area decades ago after his da committed suicide. His ma disowned him, according to the sarge. He knew him from school. Said they were friends once, but that he was a bad sort."

"I didn't realise Jock's father had killed himself. Did your sergeant say why that was?"

"Phil – the man you know as Jock – McGuire's ma kicked his da out after the neighbours told her he was sheep rustling."

Marjorie felt her eyebrows rise. "My, my… that's a term you don't hear every day."

"Maybe not, but there were a lot of sheep farms in these parts back then, and farmers didn't take kindly to McGuire's sort."

"Did they have proof it was Mr McGuire Senior?" Marjorie asked.

"You're astute, Mrs Snellthorpe, I'll give you that. I asked the same question but was told it wasn't relevant to the investigation."

Marjorie thought it might be highly relevant – particularly so if Jock's father was innocent. No wonder the man was so bitter against the locals. She had an idea his accusers might have been on Jock's target list and therefore her suspect list. She didn't mention any of this to Frankie, but asked, "How was he murdered?"

"Pathologist says he was struck twice. Once on the back of the head, which probably took him by surprise, and then the fatal blow came from the front. We'll know more after a thorough autopsy."

"Would he have suffered?" As much as she hadn't taken to Jock McGuire, it still seemed a horrible way to die.

"Don't you worry yourself aboot that. I doubt he knew too much aboot it." Frankie grinned at her with twinkling eyes. "Now you've interviewed me, it might be time for me to ask you some questions."

Marjorie chuckled. "You'll have to excuse an inquisitive old woman. It's all those Agatha Christie novels I've read. Sometimes curiosity gets the better of me."

"You'd have made a good copper. You weren't one, were you?"

"Goodness me, no. My key role in life was that of a successful businessman's wife. Entertaining was my forte."

Frankie's lips turned upwards. "And I expect you were very good at it; you've got an easy way aboot yer."

"Thank you. I shall take that as a compliment. I've never found a body before, though. Now, what is it you would like to know?"

"First off; did you see anything or anyone acting suspicious before or after you found him?"

Marjorie scrunched her eyes, trying to recall the events of the walk. "I thought I heard something in the woods in the moments before I stumbled upon Mr McGuire… oh… and there was the roar of a car engine heading away. I think that was the Lamborghini owned by—"

"Mrs Brown-Jones."

"Quite," said Marjorie. "Then I heard footsteps heading in my direction. That turned out to be Mick Burns. I called out when I found Mr McGuire. At first, I thought someone had fallen over. It was a little slippery on the path; it was only later I wondered if he had been murdered. I'm sure you've been told this already, but he kept going on about how he was writing a book – an Exposé – he told my travelling companion. He ranted a little about how people would be made to pay. To be honest, I thought he was paranoid and trying to big-up his book, but now you've told me about his father. Who knows? Perhaps he blamed those people for his death. In the brief dealings I had with him, I recognised a very bitter man. It's difficult to say anything other than he was unpleasant. Arriving under an assumed name wasn't fair to our welcoming hotelier. She got quite a shock. I apologise, I've gone off the point, haven't I?"

Frankie took copious notes but looked up at that point. "What makes you think he upset Nessa, erm… the proprietor?"

"Poor Nessa appeared startled; frightened even when she saw him. She made it clear she wasn't expecting him and told him the hotel was full. He – rather maliciously, I have to say – pointed to the new first name, acquired on purpose, I should imagine, as an element of surprise."

"I see." Frankie's jaw clenched. "What made you feel she was frightened?"

"Her reaction. She went from warm and friendly to running scared. The poor woman didn't hang around at all afterwards and – this is only my opinion – spent the rest of the day avoiding him. His manner with her was threatening. If I'd been her, I would have been unsettled too. I'm rambling; it probably isn't relevant at all."

Frankie relaxed. "Perhaps not, but thanks for the insight. When you said you heard someone in the woods, did you see who it was, and could you tell whether it was a man or a woman?"

"I can't say for certain what I heard was human," said Marjorie. "It could have been an animal. I thought a twig cracked, but anything else; I don't know." She didn't mention having the feeling of being watched, as she didn't want the kind detective to put her down as a neurotic.

"Aye, it could've been an animal. They get foxes, deer, rabbits and all sorts in these parts. Thank you, Mrs Snellthorpe. You've been helpful. I'll get this lot typed up later and you can sign it. Would you mind writing yer full name and address, please? Save me asking the proprietor; she's probably had enough for one day."

"With pleasure," said Marjorie.

Frankie's eyes widened. "Sorry, I've been calling you Mrs and I should have been calling you Lady."

"Not at all. Most people call me Marjorie and I'd be happy for you to do so. Do you mind if I make a suggestion?"

"Go on."

"I think the answer to Jock... or Phil... McGuire's death might lie in his book. Has anyone searched his room?"

"Not yet. The DI wanted us to wait until she's finished at the scene, then she'll be up here to take a look. Speaking of that, I'd better get back down there and see what's what."

"Does your DI normally spend so long at a crime scene?" Marjorie asked, feeling it was unusual to be so hands-on.

"I couldn't say." Frankie jumped up from his seat. "Nice talking to yer, Lady Marjorie," he gave her a wide grin before leaving the room.

Marjorie got up to leave and noticed an old photograph on a bookshelf to the side of the desk. The young woman in the photo was Nessa, and she assumed the couple standing on either side were her parents. If so, the father was gazing adoringly at his daughter, who was laughing. Marjorie thumbed the picture. Such a shame she ever got mixed up with a certain Phil McGuire. The photo must have been taken after she married, as Nessa's left hand bore a wedding ring. Marjorie peered closer to see if there was a date.

"That's the last picture we had taken as a family. My mammy got depressed and hardly left the house a few months after it was taken."

Marjorie was pleased she hadn't been holding the photo, otherwise she would have dropped it. "I'm so sorry, I didn't mean to intrude. The detective left, and I noticed the picture. I can't resist photographs. I'm sorry to hear about your mother. Depression can be an awful thing."

"Aye, it can." Nessa moved towards the photograph and wiped it with a handkerchief. "How are you feeling? I hope you've recovered from the shock of this morning."

"I'm well. Thank you for asking. The loch outing was therapeutic."

"What did Frank have to say?"

"They're treating the death as murder, but you most likely gathered that from the police presence down near the loch."

"Yes, some of the guests have been down there trying to have a nose."

"We met his sergeant. Officious man."

"I know who you mean, Bill Bell. I'd stay away from him if I were you, he's a right old misery. He was just as miserable as a child, but then, if your nickname was Wally William, you could well be miserable." Nessa laughed.

"I suppose I might be. We crossed paths near the crime scene when I asked if they could move their van away from your entrance. The coach couldn't turn in."

"You'll know what I mean then. Brian told me the entrance was blocked. He came in the back way. There's a small track that leads off the north side of the hotel and comes out next to our neighbours. I almost forgot… the rest of your crew is asking after you. They told me to let you know they were in the bar."

"Thank you." Marjorie realised she was being dismissed. With forehead furrowed, she soon found Edna, Horace and Frederick sitting around a table having a hushed conversation.

Chapter 22

Frederick pulled out a seat for Marjorie when he saw her arriving. "Sorry we left you down there, but Edna was getting cold."

Put out more like, thought Marjorie. "As it turned out, we got a lift back with a rather handsome young detective."

"Horace told us – he didn't mention the handsome part, though!" Frederick's eyes danced with mischief. "How was the interview?"

"You don't have to whisper. You know we want to know too," bellowed Edna.

"And you don't need to shout when I'm only a few inches away," said Marjorie, giving Horace a friendly wink.

Edna folded her arms. "I wasn't shouting."

A truce was required before they went off track, with Edna in this kind of mood. Marjorie turned to ask Brian, who she noticed hovering out of the corner of her eye, for a pot of tea. "We need to be more circumspect when that man is around. He pops up everywhere," she explained.

"You're right, he does," Edna conceded. "I hadn't even noticed him standing there. I hope he didn't hear what we were discussing."

Marjorie looked around before asking. "And what was it you were discussing that was so interesting you didn't see him?"

"Edna and I had a mooch in the late Jock McGuire's room," said Frederick, beaming.

They stopped talking for a moment when Brian reappeared with the tea. Marjorie made sure he and anyone else were out of hearing distance as crowds were making their way in from the coach. Lowering her voice, she asked. "Did you find anything significant? A certain manuscript, for instance? Frankie, the detective constable, told me the police hadn't been into the room yet."

"No, someone got to it before we did," said Edna.

"I'd have been surprised if they hadn't," said Marjorie. "I would imagine the killer would have come up here before or after the murder to remove whatever was in that book."

"There's nothing passes you by, Marjorie," said Horace.

"His laptop had gone too," said Frederick, "so assuming he didn't have a copy with a publisher, it's all gone."

"It appears Jock was intending to leave this morning, though."

"Shall I tell the story or would you like to take over?" Edna snapped at Horace, who leaned back in his chair, palms open.

"Sorry, go ahead."

"His suitcase was on the bed, the lock had been broken, and his stuff was strewn all over the room. Whoever was in there had been in a hurry, so much so they didn't even try to hide the fact. What makes you think they went in around the time of the murder, by the way?" Edna's eyes narrowed.

"Presumably because they – like the rest of us – would have assumed, if the police were called, they would have checked the room much earlier in the day."

"Yes, it's weird they haven't done that yet," said Frederick. "It's the first thing I would have done as the investigating officer."

Edna shot him a look of disdain. "You! An investigating officer; now that I'd like to see. You didn't even want to come up to the room in the first place."

Frederick's head flushed along with his cheeks. "Only because we didn't have permission or the authority to do so. What if they had caught us? The police might have thought it was us that ransacked the room – or worse – committed the murder. We could have been arrested."

"The man's got a point, Edna," said Horace, getting a glowering response.

"What is this? Pick on Edna day?"

"Perhaps the police haven't realised the significance of the book just yet," said Marjorie, not wanting to lose track. "Frankie told me Jock's father committed suicide after being accused of sheep rustling. The sergeant doesn't believe that's significant, but it could explain Jock's bitterness."

"Did I hear you right, sheep rustling?" Horace chortled.

Even Edna smirked. "They're very old-fashioned up here, aren't they?"

"This happened over thirty years ago, I think, and I expect it is important if you depend on sheep for your livelihood."

"Marjorie makes a good point," said Horace.

"Here we go again. Marge this, Marge that. I don't know why I bother."

Ignoring Edna's sulk, Marjorie asked. "Did you find anything else in the room that might tell us who was responsible?"

Edna shot Horace another glare before answering. "I found some notes under the lining of the suitcase."

"It was my idea," said Frederick. "I like to watch spy films and they always check the linings."

"Where are these documents?" Marjorie asked.

Edna harrumphed. "Mr Spy here made us leave them behind, but was clever enough to take photos on his phone. The only thing is, he can't take a decent picture; they're useless, blurred."

The corners of Frederick's mouth drooped as he wiped his brow with a handkerchief. "I'm not cut out for all this cloak-and-dagger stuff. I was so worried about being caught my hands must have been shaking when I was taking them. Not only that, I didn't manage to take snaps of all the sheets."

"So, thanks to James Bond here, our search was a complete waste of time," said Edna, casting Frederick a scathing look. "I'd have been better on my own."

"And would you have thought to check the suitcase lining?" Marjorie asked.

"Maybe not," Edna conceded.

"At least we know there are some notes there. I wonder if we should risk another foray?"

"Alas, that won't be possible," said Horace. "Frankie took the key before leaving the hotel, and we can hardly ask to borrow the master key."

"Never mind. We just have to accept the police will find the notes rather than us. Let's hope they lead them to the murderer. At least the killer doesn't know of their existence or where they are." Despite trying to sound chipper, Marjorie was disappointed at their lack of progress. Inwardly, she enjoyed crime solving, but had to accept she had been lucky in the past and acknowledged that one day her luck might run out.

"Did you learn anything else from Frankie?" Horace asked.

"Not really. The only interesting fact was that the miserable sergeant we met had grown up around here and knew the dead man. The DI's fairly new, and English. We already know the local policewoman is from out of this area, so the investigation should remain unbiased."

"I'm still surprised no-one has searched his room," Horace said.

"It appears the DI is the hands-on type. I expect she wants to be present when they do," said Marjorie.

"Or she doesn't trust her sergeant," said Frederick. "If he knew McGuire, he's unlikely to have much sympathy. The man was not the life and soul of the party and all that."

Marjorie sipped her second cup of tea. "From what Horace and I saw of the sergeant, I wouldn't have thought he was that popular either. For all we know, Jock – or rather, Phil McGuire – might have been his type. Frankie said they were school friends, but the sergeant, Bill Bell, told him he was bad news."

"Bill Bell? Bloomin' 'eck, what sort of name is that?" quizzed Edna.

"A better one than his nickname. He was known as Wally William at school," Marjorie giggled.

"No wonder he's so miserable. I bet this lot knows him as well then," said Horace.

"I'm sure they do," agreed Marjorie.

"It makes sense not to send him up here on his own. Did the handsome Frankie say why they were taking so long down there?" Frederick asked.

"He didn't know, or wasn't saying. He told me the pathologist said two blows to the head caused the death. Back and front."

"Ouch," said Horace. "Maybe they're short on forensics; he's hardly going to admit that."

Marjorie's mind was wandering back to something else which she felt was significant but couldn't quite grasp. A bit like Frederick's blurred photos, there was something at the back of her mind, but the focus wasn't there.

Chapter 23

Dinner was a rather flat affair. Horace and Frederick were preoccupied from the moment Grace Brown-Jones entered the room, which left Edna unable to control the poisoned barbs headed in the other woman's direction. Marjorie was deep in thought.

The police hovered around in the lobby having drinks.

"They don't seem in any hurry, do they?" Marjorie remarked.

"Who?" asked Horace.

"If you could drag your eyes away from the blonde, you'd know," complained Edna.

Horace's upturned lips told Marjorie he was enjoying Edna's petulance over the matter of Grace Brown-Jones. "Sorry," he said.

"The police out there. I've been watching them," said Marjorie. "They came in a good half hour ago and they still haven't been upstairs. Look at them. I think the woman's the DI."

All heads turned in the lobby's direction where Frankie, the brusque Sergeant Bell, another blonde woman – although this one was a natural – and a uniformed officer sat drinking.

"I say," said Frederick. "She's very young to be a DI."

"That's the trouble. Everyone looks too young these days." Horace sighed.

Frederick was right. The attractive woman looked to be in her late twenties at the most, but she would have to be older to have got that far, unless she was fast tracked. She was taller than her sergeant, which must grate on him almost as much as having a female boss, thought Marjorie. "DI Patricia Bloom appears to like a pint," she said out loud.

Horace opened his mouth.

"Before you say anything about women drinking from pint glasses, Horace Tyler, don't…" warned Edna.

Horace smirked. "I was going to say how refreshing it is to see a good-looking policewoman."

Edna let out a huge huff. "I despair of you, you're such a—"

"Dinosaur. You've said. You'll be saying I'm sexist next. About them having drinks, though. I suspect they need some refreshments after being down on the shore most of the day."

"What's wrong with a hot coffee?" said Edna, scathing.

"Coming from someone who drank almost a bottle of Scotch this afternoon, I'd be careful," said Horace with a wink.

"You know what I mean," Edna pouted.

"I take it you don't approve of the police drinking on duty," said Frederick.

"I don't see why they have to hog the lobby and make everyone feel uncomfortable. They should just get on with their job, find those papers, arrest someone, and get out of here, in that order."

Although Marjorie wouldn't have put it quite like Edna, she was of a similar mind, but for another reason. She wanted them to hurry up and solve the crime so she herself wouldn't feel obliged to continue investigating.

Brian cleared the table, half concentrating on his duties while keeping a close eye on the lobby. He had been particularly dour this evening.

"Can't you do something about them?" Edna nudged his elbow, nodding in the police's direction, as he took her plate.

"Nessa felt they might need a warm drink after being outside all day." He glared at the four police officers.

"They're not all on the beer, then?" Horace chuckled.

"No. Just the inspector and Frankie. The wee lad's trying to impress: cannae hold his drink at the best of times."

"You know Frankie Charles?" Marjorie's head shot up.

"Not well. Seen him aboot in the city. Goes to a pub on Young Street, so he does. I used to see him in there as a punter, and sometimes in uniform breaking up fights, but he's done well fer himself, there's no doubt aboot that."

Brian sounded almost proud of the young detective. Marjorie wondered if he would have liked a son. "We were just saying the inspector appears rather young."

Brian turned to leave. "Aye, she's got a wee bairn at home."

Marjorie suspected Horace wasn't the only one with outdated views from the disapproving tone in Brian's voice.

"I'll be back in a minute for the rest. Are youse having pudding?"

"Not for me, thanks," said Horace.

The foursome decided to leave the restaurant and head for the bar. Once seated with their drinks, Frankie and DI Bloom joined them.

"Do you mind if we join you?" The inspector had an open face and wide blue eyes. Other than a light layer of concealer, she wasn't wearing makeup. Marjorie liked her immediately.

"Not at all." Horace leapt to his feet and pulled a chair for the startled detective, who recovered and grinned.

"Thank you."

"Can I get you a drink?" Horace asked.

Marjorie noticed the beer glass was only a third drunk whereas Frankie's had been left behind, presumably empty. He glanced at the inspector for permission.

"I'm sure Frankie wouldn't mind a coffee, but I'm fine, thanks," she said.

Frankie hid his disappointment, giving Horace a half-smile. "Black please."

"I'm DI Patricia Bloom. I believe you spoke to our DC here earlier?" Patricia's eyes were firmly fixed on Marjorie's, so she replied.

"I did, but I'm not sure I can tell you anything other than what I told him."

Horace appeared back at the table with a mug of coffee.

"Take that upstairs, Frankie. You and Bell go and search Mr McGuire's room."

"Yes, ma'am."

"Tell Mahoney he can relieve the crime scene guard. Okay?"

"Will do." Frankie hesitated. "Are you sure you don't want me here, ma'am?"

"Quite sure. Off you go."

Frankie reluctantly left with his fresh brew, and moments later, he and the grumpy sergeant headed upstairs.

"Your DC didn't seem happy with his orders," said Edna. Never one to hold back an opinion.

DI Bloom grinned. "He's keen, but it can be a bit suffocating at times with all his questions," she explained. "Still, I'd rather have it that way than thinking he knows everything. And he follows orders, which is a must in my book."

Unlike Sergeant Bell, Marjorie suspected.

"Are you happy for me to ask you a few questions here, Lady Snellthorpe, or would you rather we go somewhere private?"

Marjorie scanned the bar and lobby. Nobody was paying them any attention. Either they were unaware of the reason for the police presence, or they didn't care. She checked where Grace Brown-Jones was and noticed she was being ushered into Nessa's for tête-à-tête. "As long as you call me Marjorie. The present company knows everything I do and I can't see that anything I have to say would interest anyone else."

Marjorie introduced the other three members of the quartet. Edna gave a curt nod while Horace and Frederick were welcoming. After the introductions, she said. "Now please, ask away."

Chapter 24

Marjorie retold her story from leaving the hotel to arriving at the shore, including the sensation that someone might have been watching her, and ending with her discovery of the deceased Jock McGuire. Patricia Bloom listened carefully, checking her notes and occasionally interrupting to seek clarification or further information. Marjorie warmed to the attentive young inspector, as she had done to Frankie.

Patricia's intense blue eyes scrutinised Marjorie. "You mentioned feeling you were being watched. From what direction?"

"It's hard to say. I heard movement in the woods on my right, moments before hearing footsteps coming my way, and before finding Mr McGuire, who I initially thought had fallen."

Patricia left the table for a moment and spoke into her radio. On return she explained, "Our forensics' team has been doing a fingertip search of the area all day. They covered the area you mentioned and found nothing untoward."

"Well, they wouldn't, would they?" Edna had been quiet, but was growing impatient at being left out of the conversation. "It was bucketing it down. Any evidence would have been washed away by now."

"I'm not saying there was no-one there, just if there was, they left no evidence."

"Oh," said Edna, flushing. "No muddy boot prints, then?"

"Sadly not. The wood in that area is covered in rocks and moss. It leads into the hill on which this hotel is built. I'm told it's quite treacherous if you don't know what you're doing."

"But doesn't it lead to the road?" Marjorie asked.

"Yes, eventually, but that part of the road is higher up. The safest route is via the path or the shore back to the road you entered across from the hotel track and where our cordon's in place. I believe you know where that is." The left side of Patricia's mouth turned upwards, eyes teasing.

Marjorie grinned. "Sorry about that."

"No problem. We shouldn't have left the van where we did. Sergeant Bell doesn't agree. He thinks you were fishing."

"I hate fishing. That was my husband's hobby." Marjorie chuckled.

"Our presence rather put your Sergeant Bell out," said Horace, joining the conversation.

DI Bloom rolled her eyes, opened her mouth, but clamped it shut again. Marjorie suspected she had been about to say something derogatory about her sergeant, but changed her mind.

"He was right in part," said Marjorie. "I must admit, I am interested in the investigation. I didn't tell young Frankie this, but Jock McGuire told me yesterday he thought someone might try to kill him."

"Did you believe him?"

"Not at the time, no. I thought he was a rather odd man, and paranoid to boot. He appeared intent on telling everyone he met about the book he was writing and seemed to enjoy upsetting people. Especially those he knew from his younger days."

"That's very astute of you to notice," said the DI.

"It didn't take much deduction," complained Edna. "The man argued with just about everyone he met. *We* believe it was something in that book got him killed."

Marjorie grinned inwardly at Edna, now emphasising the word 'we'.

"He was an unpleasant man. Fred here had a word with him about upsetting the ladies," said Horace.

"And the men," Edna sniped.

"What kind of word?" DI Bloom's line of questioning was now intent on weighing up their little group.

"I just asked him if he would be willing to stop creating tension, that's all. And my name's Frederick." He shot a sulking look towards Horace.

"And how did he take your suggestion, *Frederick*?" asked DI Bloom.

"Not as bad as I'd expected. First, he told me to mind my own business, but after chatting for a little while, he changed. He said his work here was done and he would check out this morning. To be honest, I wondered if he was just spending time trying to stir up interest in his book. His suitcase..." Frederick's eyes widened and darted towards Edna.

"We heard him saying he would pack his suitcase first thing," Edna came to the rescue. Marjorie noticed Frederick's bald head redden, and he leaned down to rub a shin which had obviously taken a kick from his saviour.

"Mm," DI Bloom rubbed her right cheekbone with a rough hand, out of keeping with the rest of her appearance. "The owner, Vanessa Wallace, confirms he told the night receptionist he would check out today."

"What night receptionist?" Horace asked what Marjorie had been about to do . "I didn't see anyone, and I was up late."

"You told me you were going to bed," Edna snapped.

"Couldn't sleep, so I got up again and went downstairs for a drink. The bar was shut and so was the reception. In fact, it would have been pitch black, but for a full moon. I sat at the bar and had a dip from my private supply." Horace tapped his inside breast pocket where he carried a small bottle of Scotch.

"And what time was this?" DI Bloom asked.

"Around midnight. I remember thinking it was witching hour when I looked at the moon."

"Don't say stuff like that. It's bad enough being so close to the loch," Edna nudged Horace's arm.

"Don't tell me you believe in witches and the Loch Ness Monster?" Frederick gawped.

"Just because we don't see everything, don't mean it ain't there." Edna folded her arms, glaring around, challenging anyone to argue with her.

DI Bloom's mischievous eyes told Marjorie, had she not been in the middle of a murder investigation, she might have something to say, but instead turned back to Marjorie. "I don't suppose Mr McGuire gave you any clues as to who might try to kill him?"

"Alas. No. As I said, until this morning, I thought he was being irrational. He liked the sound of his own voice. I felt he was up here on some kind of vendetta."

"Against whom?"

"Nessa, for one," said Edna. "She was his ex."

"I know about their previous relationship, but that was a long time ago. They both moved on and married."

"So there's a widow?" Marjorie caught on.

"No. There was a wife, but she and Mr McGuire divorced two years ago. She's still his next of kin. They didn't have children, and he listed her name with the tour guide."

"The other people he upset were Mick Burns and that big fella, Brian," said Horace.

"I think Brian's just protective of Nessa, but if they had both moved on…" Marjorie wasn't certain Jock McGuire wouldn't bear a grudge if he felt he had been used. "There's also Gemma Stewart."

"Who is?" DI Bloom asked.

"The wife of the head gardener. He was arguing with them yesterday. Gemma was on the boat trip today, observing us the whole time we were in the cabin."

"Now who's being paranoid?" mocked Edna. "And… Aren't we forgetting someone?

"Go on," DI Bloom grinned at Edna.

"*The blonde,*" she cackled as Horace looked on in horror.

Chapter 25

Before DI Bloom could ask any more questions, Frankie appeared and pulled up a seat.

"Where's Bell?" DI Bloom asked.

"He's gone down to the crime scene to check on Mahoney."

"Couldn't he have done that by radio?" The inspector splayed the palms of her hands on the table, taking a deep breath.

"He's cheesed off we didn't do the room search earlier."

"Why?"

"Somebody else got there first. The room's a mess… looks like Mr McGuire had packed to leave, but everything in his suitcase's been disturbed."

"I guess that means you didn't find the infamous book that could lead us to our killer?" DI Bloom pushed a tongue into her cheek before sucking in both cheeks.

The quartet looked on expectantly, waiting for Frankie to reveal what they already knew.

"We didn't find a thing," Frankie said flatly, breaking eye contact with his boss. "The sarge says if we'd—"

"I can well imagine what Sergeant Bell said," Patricia Bloom snapped for the first time since they had met her.

Frederick and Marjorie exchanged confused looks. Edna opened and closed her mouth.

"Thank you for your time, Marjorie. I think it's time I looked at this room for myself. Let's go." The inspector left her half-drunk pint on the table and strode across the lobby towards the stairs with Frankie trotting behind. Marjorie heard the DI bark. "And get that man on the radio. Now!"

"Yes ma'am."

"I don't think she's too pleased about her sour sergeant doing a bunk," said Horace. "I can't blame her. He obviously doesn't enjoy having a woman in charge."

"Perhaps he's one of those men who doesn't like obeying orders at all," said Marjorie. "I suspect Patricia Bloom isn't a walkover."

"You could be right. Maybe his last boss was more forgiving." Horace said.

"Never mind about all that. Why haven't they found the papers? Are they blind?" Edna snapped.

"I expect the sergeant's a oneupmanship kind of guy and didn't put too much effort into the search once they discovered the room had been ransacked. Probably quite pleased to be able to accuse his inspector of incompetence," Frederick suggested.

"It is surprising she didn't have the room searched earlier. Perhaps she had her reasons," said Marjorie. "Other than that, I like her and believe she's more savvy than Sergeant Bell realises."

"Frankie's too busy trying to play both sides and, I suspect, cosying up for his own gain. He needs to focus. They wouldn't have found the papers unless they did what we did and explored under the lining," said Frederick.

"I expect you're right," said Marjorie. "I'm sure Inspector Bloom will be more thorough than her sergeant was."

Edna's face flushed to match the red wig she was wearing. "Erm…"

"What?" asked Marjorie.

"I didn't put the papers back where I found them. Only an idiot would fail to see them."

As all eyes rounded on Edna, Marjorie rubbed her crinkled forehead. "Someone else went into the room after you left."

"The killer," suggested Horace.

"Why didn't you put them where you found them?" Frederick's eyes widened as he shook his head.

"Because you, Mr bloomin' Cowardy Pants, kept going on about how we shouldn't be in there after taking your useless photos, so don't look at me like I'm the one who's to blame."

"There, there, Edna," said Horace. "Nobody's to blame; you both did your best. As Marjorie says, someone should have searched the room much earlier in the day. It's not our fault the police didn't do their job properly. Let me get you a Scotch."

Marjorie noticed a single tear form in the corner of Edna's eye, so she said nothing else about the carelessness. "You weren't to know the killer would return to the room. I wonder why they did that?"

"They must have seen us," said Frederick.

"Or heard you crowing," shot Edna.

Frederick lowered his eyes to the floor before looking bashfully at Marjorie. "To be honest, we were a bit excited when we came back down here. I guess someone could have overheard us talking about the find."

"We!" Edna chirped. "You couldn't stop going on about how clever you were, taking photos of the papers. Until you got your stupid phone out and showed me the pathetic blurs."

"Not to mention you letting everyone in the hotel know what an idiot I was," Frederick retorted.

Marjorie's heart sank into her stomach. "Stop arguing and consider. Who was in the lobby when you had this, erm… discussion?"

"Everyone," said Frederick, looking around desperately to check no-one was listening to them now. They were alone in the bar. "Nessa walked by, Mick Burns was sitting at the bar, Brian served us coffee. The gardener was watering plants. They were all here."

"You forgot to mention *the blonde*." Edna's eyes narrowed. "As if you wouldn't have noticed her. She was sitting at the table next to us with the gardener's wife."

"Lordy," said Marjorie. "So it could have been any of them who went to the room after hearing you. Did you see any of them leave?"

Frederick looked down again. "We left first. Edna wanted to change her wig, and I went for a quick shower. When I came down, she and Horace were already here. Almost as soon as we'd finished telling him about our expedition, you arrived."

"We'll have to come clean with the inspector, but first of all, I suggest we have a stronger drink, and I'm buying." Marjorie's heart filled with dread when she was stopped in her tracks by a blood-curdling scream.

Chapter 26

The scream and further commotion came from the gardens at the front of the hotel. Chairs clattered and chaos ensued as people rushed outside to see what had happened. Mick Burns's daughter sat on a bench being consoled by her fiancé. Mick was crouched over someone lying on the ground. Marjorie couldn't see who it was because a crowd of panic-stricken guests had gathered round and were all talking at once.

Horace stepped into the fray, moving people aside as he did so. Marjorie took her opportunity to stay close.

"Step aside, please," Horace's authoritative voice commanded obedience and people did as he said.

Marjorie gasped.

"Has anyone called an ambulance?" Horace yelled. Everyone looked at each other as if it ought to be someone else's responsibility.

"I'll do it now," Brian shouted from the steps before heading back inside.

"Tell the police while you're at it. They went up to Jock McGuire's room," Horace called, but Brian was already gone.

Mick's fingers were fumbling around the man's neck before he looked up. "There's a pulse. Tell that ambulance to hurry. He's fading fast."

Moments later, DI Bloom and Frankie Charles arrived on the scene. Marjorie caught Patricia Bloom's arm. "It's your sergeant. It's bad."

"Get these people to stand back, Frankie," Patricia Bloom instructed.

Frankie's eyes bulged when he saw his colleague lying on the frosty lawn.

"Now! Frankie." Bloom gave him a nudge.

While Frankie held both arms out, shepherding the guests back behind an imaginary line, Marjorie and Horace were allowed to stay. Mainly because Horace appeared to know some first aid and he and Mick pulled Sergeant Bell onto his side into the recovery position.

"He's alive," said Horace. "Just…"

Bloom exhaled before getting on the radio. "Get me an air ambulance to Nessie's Lochside Hotel, stat." She turned to Marjorie. "Help is on its way. Who found him?"

"Looking at the state of Mick's daughter, I think she did." Marjorie inclined her head towards the young couple on the bench. The young woman was now wrapped in a blanket, drinking something.

Mick looked up. "Aye, Shelagh tripped over him. Poor girl's in shock."

Patricia knelt down to check on her sergeant, feeling his chest, which was moving in and out. Marjorie noticed a pool of blood behind where Horace and Mick had turned the man.

"Frankie! Get the bleed kit out the van."

Frankie was statuesque, staring at the scene with the crowd behind him. "The what?"

"Never mind. I'll do it myself. Make sure there's space for a helicopter to land." DI Bloom was back moments later with a dressing in her shaking hand. "Do either of you know how to use one of these?"

"I do," said Mick, taking the pack from her hand. He unwrapped the package and removed a bloodstained towel, which he must have asked for before they arrived. He applied the special haemostatic dressing, followed by a pressure bandage.

The whirring of helicopter blades and the draft it created as it moved in to land was a welcome sound and feeling.

"That was quick," said Marjorie.

"The air ambulance is based at Inverness airport," explained Patricia Bloom.

Frederick took charge, shepherding the crowd back, as Frankie was still motionless. "Stay back everyone. Don't get underneath the chopper."

Marjorie watched on as the doctor and paramedics took a brief history from Mick and Horace. DI Bloom did her best to stop them trampling the crime scene but realised it was hopeless and let them get on with it. Within minutes,

Sergeant Bell was on a stretcher and aboard the ambulance helicopter. The doctor congratulated Mick and Horace on their swift action.

"It was the inspector who gave us the bleed kit," said Horace.

"But you put him in the recovery position. You might have saved this man's life." The doctor boarded the helicopter, followed by a resurgent Frankie.

"Where the hell are you going?" DI Bloom shouted.

"I need to be with him, ma'am." Frankie's eyes were streaming.

"No, Constable. You need to be here with me. We have a murder, an attempted murder, and now we're without a sergeant. Get down from there."

The doctor yelled to be heard above the helicopter blades. "We need to go."

DI Bloom ran towards the helicopter and grabbed Frankie's wrists. "I know you're upset, but you have to stay here." In a gentler voice she said, "I'll phone ahead and have an officer meet the helicopter in case he wakes up."

Frankie didn't move.

"Get off that helicopter before I pull you off," DI Bloom's tone shook the young man out of his stupor.

He looked from Bell to his DI, then patted the sergeant's arm. "Hang on in there, pal." He jumped from the helicopter and Patricia Bloom pulled him away so the aircraft could take off.

A sullen Frankie watched the light of the chopper fade into the distance. With Bell on his way to the hospital, DI

Bloom was back in charge. "Get a cordon set up around here, Frankie. I'll start taking statements." She turned to the crowd, some of whom were making their way towards the hotel. "I want everyone to stay in the hotel lobby until one of us has taken a statement. No-one is to leave the hotel for any reason."

Marjorie heard some mutterings and mumblings, but her eyes were on the wretched figure of Frankie Charles. He was going to be of little use to the inspector. She and the others were going to have to step up. She moved towards Patricia Bloom, who was heading over to the young couple. "I don't think DC Charles is quite with it yet. Would you like us to take a list of names and where people were around the time your sergeant was attacked? We could also search the grounds for a possible weapon."

"Lady Snellthorpe. I thank you for your help earlier, but I'm trying to conduct a murder investigation. Please understand me when I say this is not amateur detective night."

"Quite," said Marjorie. "I apologise." She turned to Horace, lowering her voice. "It looks as though we're on our own. He's going to be of no use whatsoever, and our inspector might be good, but she's too proud to realise she needs our help."

"You're right. Poor Frankie's in shock. Such a friendly fellow, too."

"Judging by his reaction, he may have chosen the wrong profession."

"Frankie!" Inspector Bloom's voice bellowed from the bench at the constable, who was still staring into the night sky.

He turned. "What?"

"Cordon," she yelled. "Get on with it and call Mahoney up here to help. I'll radio the station and ask for a replacement and get some more uniforms."

Frankie dropped the sullen teenager behaviour and snapped out of his trance. "Righto, ma'am. I'm on it."

***

Edna was sitting inside with a glass of Scotch. "Well, thanks very much, you lot. I got shoved back into the crowd while you were all playing the hero out there."

"I was with you," said Frederick.

"Yeah, until you started playing muster commander and landing sergeant."

"I didn't feel the young policeman was coping, that's all." Frederick turned to Horace and Marjorie. "He wasn't keeping order. If it hadn't been for me, the crowd would have inched forward, so I felt I had to step in."

Horace tapped Frederick on the shoulder. "Quite right, Fred. I'd have done the same. Don't look like that, Edna; we've got work to do. The inspector has told Marjorie to mind her own business." That and a wink from Horace did the trick.

Edna grinned. "Really?"

"Not quite, but that was her meaning. I don't think she realises she can't do everything by herself. At least she's called for reinforcements."

"Like someone else I know," said Edna, cackling.

Horace snorted. "I suggest we order a round of drinks and move into the conservatory. Drink up, Edna. I'll get you a refill."

"We were told to stay in the lobby," Frederick protested.

"Since when do we obey orders?" said Marjorie, grinning.

"Yeah. Lighten up, Fred," said Edna. "It's too noisy in here anyway. I can't hear myself think since this lot came in."

"Where's Faith?" Horace asked.

"She's doing the rounds, trying to placate an angry group of guests who want to go to bed. Here she is now," said Edna.

"In view of past experience, I probably don't need to ask if you're okay," Faith half-smiled. "What is it about the four of you and murder?"

"Don't look at me," said Frederick. "I'm still in awe of these three, especially Marjorie."

"Humph," said Edna.

"You can't get out of it that easily. To me, you're the awesome foursome from now on. I shouldn't really make light of the situation; it's another tragedy." Faith looked around, wistful. "Anyway, is there anything I can get you?"

"Why don't you join us for a drink? Horace is just about to get a round in." Marjorie suggested.

Faith flopped down on a chair. "Actually, I could do with a brandy and soda if you don't mind. I've spoken to everyone in our party apart from Mick and his two."

"They're still outside on the terrace," said Frederick.

"Right. Two brandies, one with soda. I take it that's what you would like, Marjorie. Scotches for me and Edna. What about you, Fred?"

"Brandy, please," Frederick answered, but not before giving an eye roll.

"Do you have any idea what happened out there?" Faith asked.

"From what I've gathered. Sergeant Bell left in a huff after he and Frankie – that's the DC – had searched Jock McGuire's room. About twenty minutes later, we heard a scream coming from outside. By the time we got there, a crowd had gathered. Shelagh Burns had obviously stumbled – quite literally, from what we heard – over the sergeant lying on the lawn. It's odd there was no lighting on outside. I'm sure there was last night." Marjorie stopped speaking for a moment while Horace placed drinks on the table. "What I don't understand is why Jock McGuire's killer would attack the sergeant. It makes little sense."

"Perhaps he bumped into the attacker and noticed the papers taken from Jock's room," Edna said.

"What papers?" Faith asked.

"That's another story," said Marjorie, glaring at Edna. "And one we don't really have time to go into right now, but it's plausible that the sergeant could have come across the killer."

"Maybe those papers were in the room after all, and he worked out who the killer was, but wanted to leave the inspector out and take all the credit." Horace said. "He's the type from the little we saw of him. An arrogant misogynist, if you ask me."

Edna's jaw dropped. "Takes one to know one, Horace Tyler."

"I might be old-fashioned, Edna Parkinton, but I don't consider myself a misogynist. I like women."

"True," Edna conceded.

"The sergeant didn't appear to like his inspector, but we can't be certain it's because she's a woman. I suspect he has an authority problem."

"So you said before," said Edna.

"I can't believe he would pocket evidence, though, and I'm sure Frankie would have known about it if he had," said Marjorie.

"In which case, we're back to him stumbling across the killer outside or working it out in some other way. Perhaps he was trying to make the arrest when he got clobbered."

"Do you think he'll live?" Faith asked.

Horace frowned. "Hard to say. He took quite a bang to the head. From the amount of blood lost, the attacker left him for dead. According to Mick, even if he lives, there might be severe trauma to the brain. Good thing he knew a bit of first aid or the man might have died at the scene."

"Was it his suggestion to put him in the recovery position?" Marjorie asked.

"No. That was mine. We put on regular first aid courses in the firm and I drop in every so often."

"If he knew so much, why hadn't he already done that?" Edna put into words what Marjorie had been thinking.

"He was worried about moving him in case of other injuries, but I told him that would be irrelevant if the guy choked on his own tongue. Sometimes you can get bleeding from the nose into the throat as well, and the sergeant would not have been able to cough in his unconscious state."

"All of which I would have thought Mick Burns would know," said Marjorie.

"Are you suggesting he didn't want to help?" Frederick asked. "Or that he's our killer?"

"It's hard to say. His daughter was severely traumatised, so he might not have been thinking straight," Marjorie replied. "One thing I am certain of, and that is our killer was there and watching on, and he or she knows that Sergeant Bell is alive."

"Meaning they might try again," said Edna.

"Just when I thought things couldn't get any worse," said Faith, draining her glass. "I'd better get back to work. It's looking like it could be a long night."

207

After she had gone, Marjorie said, "And we had better get back to work too. At least our killer's going nowhere tonight."

Chapter 27

The quartet arrived in the conservatory to find a young couple wrapped in each other's arms. One look from Edna was all it took to make them scarper. It was useful having Edna around sometimes to clear a room, Marjorie conceded.

"What are our tour plans for tomorrow?" Frederick asked.

"Two murders and all you can think about is your jollies." Edna fired one of her most pointed looks in Frederick's direction.

"One murder," he corrected. "You know how I feel about these things. We should leave such matters to the police. I hope we don't get arrested when we tell the inspector what we did, and judging by her mood since someone attacked her sergeant, I think it's a distinct possibility."

"Fred's got a point there," said Horace, "but I think the inspector's got her hands full for now, unless she can get help."

"That's why it's incumbent upon us to assist her in any way we can. She needs us even if she doesn't realise it," said Marjorie.

Frederick let out a heavy sigh. "I surrender. What's the plan?"

"First, did you or Edna get a look at the papers you found? Were there any words that stuck out while you were taking photographs, for instance?"

Frederick took a gulp of brandy, forehead crinkled. "Not really. The notes were handwritten. I think it was like his book outline. I remember seeing a couple of headings." He rubbed his eyes.

"Well? What were they?" Edna prodded, impatience getting the better of her.

"I'm trying to think. I can't think under pressure... Oh, now I recall... there was one heading that stood out: Village Slut."

"That's interesting. I wonder if that's a reference to Nessa? The one who broke his heart, such as it was," Marjorie postulated.

"But they both remarried," said Horace.

"Yes, but we saw how she reacted to him when he arrived and how menacing he was with her. I don't think he was the type of man who would forgive anyone for breaking up with him. Perhaps he moved on but didn't move on, if that makes any sense?" Marjorie tried to recall every moment where she had seen Jock McGuire from the airport, up until the meeting in the woods. A shiver went through her spine when she remembered how he had almost knocked her over. "He jostled me at Rogie Falls, you know. Later, following our conversation in the forest, I believe he was warning me off."

"You didn't mention that before," said Edna, folding her arms. "I told you not to wander off on your own."

"I believe you said so after my unfortunate encounter with Mr McGuire. He told me people around these parts didn't like others poking their noses into people's business. I'm almost certain he meant *his* business, and I'm also sure he bumped into me on purpose."

"You should come with a health warning, Marjorie," Horace chortled.

Marjorie grinned. "Indeed. It was later in the conversation he mentioned someone might try to kill him. At that point, I'd say he was serious and worried."

"There are two women other than Nessa he could have been referring to in that heading," Edna argued. "One of whom is more slutlike than the other."

"Now, now, Edna. If Fred or I said something like that, you'd call us sexist!"

"Stop trying to divert attention away from the facts. You know exactly who I mean."

Marjorie sensed another standoff developing, and she didn't want any petty arguments preventing them from finding out who killed Jock McGuire and attacked Sergeant Bell. "The other woman, I assume, could be

Gemma Stewart? We have little to go on regarding her, apart from the argument by the falls and her keeping us in her sights this afternoon. I suggest we need to begin by excluding each of our suspects one by one. We need someone to ask Mrs Stewart what both of those things were about. One of us should find out why Grace and Jock were arguing while we were having lunch yesterday."

"I'll speak to Grace." Both men spoke in unison.

"You're so—"

"Bloomin' obvious," Horace laughed again.

"Yeah. Anyway, I think me and Horace should speak to Gemma... casual like, and Marjorie should speak to Grace."

"What about me?" Frederick moaned.

"For someone who thinks we should leave the police to get on with their jobs, you're awful keen suddenly," Edna retorted.

"It would be most helpful if you could speak to Mick. The two of you seemed to get on yesterday. Find out where he was when his daughter came across Sergeant Bell and anything else he's not telling us," suggested Marjorie.

"You think he's the killer," said Edna.

"No, I don't, as a matter of fact. But I'd like to know why he was slow to provide appropriate treatment to Sergeant Bell. He's made it clear he knows how to apply first aid, and we witnessed it when he applied the head treatment. It's odd he didn't get on with moving the man into the recovery position, and I don't believe his explanation about not wanting to cause further damage.

He hadn't even pulled the head back to check the man's airway as far as I could see. What could be worse than suffering brain damage from lack of oxygen because of a blocked airway? Even I know that's the most important thing when someone is found unconscious."

"That to me makes him the likely perpetrator," said Horace. "Although I have to say, I hope not. I quite like the chap."

Edna's eyebrows almost hit her hairline before she shook her head.

"If it hadn't been for his daughter finding the police officer, he would be at the top of our list," said Marjorie. "But I can't see him taking that risk. He adores his daughter – you've seen the way he is with her. We all saw how upset she was."

"I also noticed he finally referred to the fake fiancé as the boyfriend," said Edna. She and Horace let out their usual joint snorts as she took Horace's arm. "Come on you. Time to get to work."

***

Edna and Horace found Gemma Stewart sitting with her husband in the lobby. She was a plain-looking woman with straight brown hair hanging just above her shoulders. Her husband was not bad looking with short sandy brown curly hair and wide brown eyes. His posture was poor, with hunched shoulders. He might have some form of scoliosis, but Edna doubted he would be as fit as he was if he did.

His face was weatherbeaten, with ruddy cheeks, whereas his wife's could do with a lot more exposure to the sun. Her complexion resembled that of a porcelain doll. They were huddled together, ignoring complaints and chatter from the other guests resenting being held in the lobby. Edna looked around. She couldn't yet see any sign of the inspector or that waste of space, Frankie. Why on earth was he in the police force? He had showed this evening he couldn't handle the pressure.

"How do you want to play this?" Horace whispered, bringing Edna out of her desired preoccupation of wanting to give Gemma some beauty tips.

"There are a couple of seats near them. I suggest we approach casually. Be subtle."

Horace squeezed her arm. "That'll be a first, Edna Parkinton."

She nudged him back. "Yeah well. I'm getting used to this undercover stuff. Come on, quick."

Edna made a beeline for the chairs, blocking the path of two men who looked as though they'd just come in from playing a round of golf, or more likely spending too much time on the nineteenth hole. She plonked herself in one seat just as the first man arrived at the other. He gave her a stare, but he and his friend headed for the bar.

"Nice one," said Horace, taking the second seat. He leaned over to where the Stewarts were and put his drink down. "You don't mind if I put my drink on your table, do you?"

Terry looked up. "Not at all. Pull your chairs up; it looks like we might be here awhile."

Gemma appeared more wary. Marjorie had said the woman had been watching them on the boat during the afternoon. Edna tried a disarming smile when she put her drink down next to Horace's.

"I'm Horace. This is Edna. Did we see you on the coach yesterday?"

Terry answered. "You did. I'm Terry, the head gardener, and this is my wife, Gemma."

Gemma gave a half-smile, but didn't make too much effort.

"Terrible business, this," Horace continued. "Do you know what happened?"

"Only that a policeman was bashed over the head. I was just telling Gemma, I overheard the young copper tell the inspector the fella who was attacked said he knew who the killer was."

"Really?" said Edna. "The inspector interviewed our friend not long before this happened. She found that other bloke dead this morning."

"Of course. I knew I'd seen you around," said Terry, who was much more friendly than his wife. "You're with Lady Marjorie."

"How did you know her title?" Edna's eyes narrowed. "She doesn't let on."

"Word gets around in a small place like this. It must have been an awful shock for her."

Edna wanted to say Marjorie didn't shock easily and was relishing this whole drama, but instead said, "It was. We noticed not so many people from these parts were that moved by it."

Terry eyed his wife warily. "That's because he had it coming."

"We realised he was an unpleasant sort," said Horace. "Seemed to argue with everyone he met. Was he always like that?"

Gemma blew out a sigh. "Aye, he was. I knew him growing up. His middle name should have been Trouble."

The mouse has a voice, thought Edna. "What about the sergeant? Did you know him?"

"Aye. He was at the same school. To be honest, he wasn't the most popular guy either, although he changed since he hooked up with…" Gemma's hand went to her mouth.

"Anyone we've met?" asked Horace.

Gemma's lips tightened. She would not say anything else on that topic. "I assume the sergeant also knew Jock McGuire?" Edna asked.

"Aye, everyone did. He was one of Phil's few friends – you've most likely been told we did not know him as Jock around here. As far as I know, the two of them had a fallout and didn't keep in touch."

"That man seemed able to fall out with his own shadow. Did he argue with you?" Edna was growing impatient with dancing round the houses and wanted this woman to just tell them what was on her mind, and what they needed to know. Instead, she got a blank stare.

"I'm going to have a word with Nessa. Find out what's going on." Gemma got up and left.

"Sorry," said Horace. "My friend obviously hit a nerve."

Terry rubbed his fists together before looking at Horace. "You weren't to know. I was completely ignorant of the man's existence before yesterday. Then he comes up to my wife at Rogie Falls and makes all sorts of threats. I told him to clear off. He's lucky I didn't belt him one."

"Why would he threaten your wife?" Edna asked.

"It was all to do with a book he was writing. Something happened to McGuire's dad, and he blamed certain people for it."

"Your wife being one of them," Horace said.

"Yep. Gemma told me about it last night. A group of them were camping as teenagers when they heard a noise. It came from a local farmhouse. You know what kids are like? They snuck out of their tents to take a look and saw McGuire Senior get in a car with someone else before driving off quick. Everything was quiet after that, and they went back to their tents. The next day, they found a couple dead in the farmhouse."

Edna sucked in her cheeks. "Are you saying Jock's dad was a murderer?"

"That's what it looked like to people at the time. But it didn't get to court. It was dark that night, and the kids couldn't be absolutely certain it was him, so he got off with it. Gemma said not long after that, McGuire was reported for something else and killed himself. Since that day, McGuire Junior has been gathering dirt on all the kids that camped that night to put in a vindictive book. He blamed them for his dad not being able to get a job in the area because of the rumours about him being a robber and a murderer. Seems Phil – Jock – couldn't accept his dad's guilt."

"I suppose the facts he's been gathering about the locals, he intended to exaggerate." Horace looked thoughtful.

Terry looked down at his half-empty glass. "He told us he knew Gemma slept with Mick Burns after the guy married. It was a one-off. Gemma told me about it before we married, but Mick's daughter knew nothing of it."

"And this fact was going in his book?" suggested Edna.

"Yep. The thing is, and don't tell Gem I told you, but she thinks Bill Bell may have been the other guy in the car that night. I'd better find her. Check she's okay." Terry rubbed his fists together again. "That man should never have come back to these parts."

Horace's wide eyes stared after Terry Stewart, lumbering away.

"Well, ain't that a turnup?" declared Edna.

Chapter 28

Marjorie walked around the room but couldn't see Grace Brown-Jones anywhere. She noticed Edna and Horace had cornered Terry and Gemma Stewart. At least someone was having success. It made her smile, listening to various groups moaning and groaning about how the police had no right to hold them like criminals. There was no sign of the object of their ire, either. DI Bloom seemed to work at her own pace and, judging by the length of time she had spent at the crime scene, it was not a quick one. Marjorie strolled towards the front doors to see if she could catch sight of Patricia Bloom or Frankie, but instead noticed the glow from a cigarette and saw Grace pacing up and down the path at the bottom of the steps. Bracing herself for the chill again, as she wasn't wearing a coat, she opened one of the doors and furtively moved outside after checking no-one was looking her way. As the door closed behind her, the peace was immediate. It was a glorious night with clear skies and a three-quarter moon, although that made the cold even more penetrating. Lights on the steps gave her enough visibility to descend.

Marjorie heard quiet sobs, but they weren't coming from Shelagh Burns. DI Bloom and her quarry had obviously moved inside.

"What on earth's the matter?"

Grace jumped before turning, then wiped her eyes aggressively with a handkerchief. "Nothing."

"It doesn't look like nothing," said Marjorie. "I don't mean to pry, dear, but you seem to be in some distress."

Grace threw the cigarette to the floor, stamping it out with a designer shoe. At any other time Marjorie would have tutted, but she kept her disapproval of littering to herself. "You'll catch your death out here. Follow me."

Unfortunate choice of words, Marjorie felt, following the taller woman around the front of the hotel. They entered again through a side door, walking along a corridor until Grace opened a door to her right. They entered a room with comfortable chairs, a television, microwave, fridge and a wall-mounted water heater. A gigantic Highland Springs water container was attached to a cold water dispenser.

"This is the staff room," Grace explained. "There won't be anyone down here for a while. Not with that commotion upstairs." Grace headed towards the hot water. "Can I get you a coffee?"

"It's a bit late for me. If there's camomile tea, I'd be grateful."

Grace opened and closed cupboards, finding something. "How about lemon and ginger?"

"That would be suitable, thank you."

Marjorie waited while Grace made them both a drink. She herself had a black coffee and handed Marjorie a mug of the herbal tea.

"Shall we sit?"

They sat down, placing mugs onto coasters laid neatly on a mahogany coffee table. The room was warm as well as snug. "This must be a nice place for the staff to relax." Marjorie didn't want to rush the woman opposite whose knee was jerking up and down at pace.

"It's far enough from the lobby to give them a proper break. The only people who use it are night staff."

Which must have been where they were this morning, thought Marjorie. "I expect daytimes are too busy."

Grace's bottom lip trembled, and she let out a loud, wailing sob.

"Please tell me what has distressed you so. Is there anything I can do to help?"

Grace got up and paced the room, at one point looking as though she might dart out through the door.

Marjorie didn't move. Not wanting to cause her to flee.

Finally, Grace stopped crying and pulled herself together enough to stutter, "It's… it's… B… Bill."

Marjorie rubbed her head before realising who she meant. "Sergeant Bell?" she asked.

Grace nodded, wiping her face with a makeup stained, wet handkerchief, the result of which was to smudge tear-lined mascara into an unsightly black splodge. "We… we…" The bottom lip went again as Grace sat down to take in some coffee.

"You were seeing each other," Marjorie finished the sentence for her.

"It must seem wrong to you, but my husband's away a lot. We barely see each other these days and have been talking about a separation for ages. We just don't get around to it and end up drifting back into the same old convenient marriage. There's a lot of joint money tied in our businesses. I guess neither of us can face the complication of dividing our assets. Too untidy." She gave a cynical laugh.

"How long have you been with Sergeant Bell, and is his wife, or your husband, aware?" Marjorie pursed her lips.

"Bill's not married. We went out together as teenagers. Six months ago, I came up here while Nessie's was being built. Nessa wanted to buy some extra land at the side. I ran into Bill when I was feeling vulnerable. He told me he had never married because he had always loved me. He told me there was no other woman like me."

I agree with that, thought Marjorie, but said. "So you rekindled the relationship."

Grace looked up at Marjorie. Eyes desperate. "It was stupid; I know that now. Bill's always wanted marriage, but he doesn't have much to offer."

"Apart from his love," Marjorie said tersely.

"Look, I enjoyed reliving my teens, but I… I don't love him, I never did. It was always about the—"

"Quite," said Marjorie, not needing to know the details of that side of things. "So, why are you so upset?"

"Because I feel so damned guilty. I called him to tell him about Jock McGuire being up here threatening to tell the world about our affair… about all my relationships, in fact. God knows how he found out."

"So Bill's not the first?"

"No. And he won't be the last, but that's beside the point. I think Bill may have killed Phil, who you know as Jock. I saw him this morning, close to where you found the body."

Marjorie raised an eyebrow, confused. "Why would he do that? Surely he'd be happy for your relationship with him to be out in the open if he wanted you to divorce?"

"To protect me. I saw him jogging in the hills. It's too much of a coincidence. He and Jock were friends once, but they had a fallout over Jock's dad."

"I heard his father committed suicide."

"Jock wouldn't let it go. He kept on saying he'd get his own back on all of us; that it was our fault his dad did what he did."

"I'm sorry, I'm not following you. Why would it be your fault?"

"Me and the others: Mick, Gemma and Nessa were camping – we were just teenagers. Brian was overseeing us with him and Mick sleeping in one tent, us girls in the other. We heard a noise in the night and went to see what it was. Brian slept through it, but Mick came out after us. We saw Jock's dad getting into a car. The others said they saw someone else there, but I think they were imagining things. After the car sped off, we went back to our tents and thought nothing of it. The next day we heard there'd been a burglary, and a couple were killed. We were pretty sure of what we'd seen, but not certain enough to get it to court and have our stories pulled apart by a good defence lawyer. Besides, none of our parents wanted us to give evidence at any trial. Villagers were very suspicious of authority. Jock... Phil's dad was persona non grata around the village after that and couldn't hold down a job. Then he was going to be charged for sheep rustling and he killed himself."

"Was Bill with you on the night you were camping?"

"No! He was nowhere near."

"How did Jock's father kill himself?"

"They found him hanging in the barn belonging to the dead couple. The case was closed after that. Sheriff's office concluded that it pointed to McGuire Senior's guilt, and that he carried out the robbery and murder."

"What about the other man?"

"The others decided they couldn't be certain they'd seen anyone else there. We were half asleep. It was dark, and we were too far away to see very much at all. That's why we wouldn't have been able to swear it was McGuire."

Marjorie felt there was something Grace wasn't telling her, but didn't want her to clam up.

"How did the couple die?"

"The guy was hit over the head, I think. It was in the papers, but my parents wouldn't let me near them. The

224

others told me his wife fell down the stairs. She must have got up when she heard her husband call out or something."

"How awful," said Marjorie, almost speechless.

"There was a real atmosphere in the village for ages afterwards."

"Getting back to Bill Bell. If he killed Jock, who do you think attacked him?"

"I… I don't know. I can't think about it anymore. It's too traumatic. What if Bill dies?"

"Do you mind if I ask you just one more question?"

"That depends what it is."

"Did anyone else know about your affair with Bill? Your husband, for instance?"

"No-one else knew. We kept it secret."

"But in a small place like this…"

"I have a bolthole in the middle of nowhere. I own property everywhere, Lady Marjorie. If I want to keep a relationship secret, I damn well know how to do it. As for my husband, he wouldn't care as long as it doesn't become public. He has his own fillies and they're not just horses. Now, if you'll excuse me, I'm going to freshen up, reapply my makeup and see if I can find out how Bill is."

After the door slammed behind her, Marjorie sat for a full twenty minutes, drinking her tea and mulling over what she had just heard. It was hard to work Grace Brown-Jones out, but one thing was clear; she cared for Bill Bell more than she was prepared to admit.

Chapter 29

Marjorie found a wild-eyed Edna marching towards her when she finally found the right passage leading up some stairs into the lobby.

"Fred and Horace are outside searching for you."

"Why?"

"Because someone said they saw you go out over an hour ago and we have not seen you since. We were worried sick. That bloomin' detective inspector wasn't interested – said she had enough to do without chasing around after people who disobeyed her instructions. She was downright rude."

"Did you tell her what we were up to?"

"I had to, otherwise she wouldn't have taken me seriously."

"Which, of course, she didn't after you told her."

"Don't you start twisting this around. The fact is, you disappeared again without telling anyone where you were going."

"I'm sorry. I ventured outside when I saw Grace smoking. She was upset and knew another way in. We went to a rather pleasant staff sitting room and had hot drinks. It was lovely…" Marjorie stopped, noticing her explanation wasn't helping her cause. She really must learn how to handle Edna better. Perhaps Horace could give her some tips. "Anyway, as you can see, I'm quite safe, but I'm close to narrowing down who the perpetrator is."

"Go on then. Spill the beans."

"Not here. Let's find the gentlemen, and then we must have a private word with Inspector Bloom."

"Good luck with that. She doesn't want to see any of us. I tried to tell her what Horace and I found out, and she as good as told me to clear off. I told young Frankie, and he wrote it all down."

"Hm. Whether or not the inspector wants to hear, she has to. We just need to find a way of getting her alone. At least there are fewer people now."

"A couple of uniformed officers arrived not long ago and have been working their way through the crowds. I still don't think that DI is in a listening mood."

"We'll worry about that later. First things first. Let's find Horace and Frederick. I don't like to think of them scouring the grounds looking for me in the freezing cold."

***

Horace came rushing in through the doors just as Marjorie and Edna were about to go in search of him and Frederick.

"Oh, there you are, Marjorie. That's a relief. We thought you might have got into trouble. Is Fred back yet?"

Frederick. Marjorie gritted her teeth. "We haven't seen him. We were just about to come and look for both of you to let you know I'm safe. Do you know which way he went?"

"He took the left, I took the right," said Horace.

"Why were you running in here like a bat out of hell?" asked Edna.

Horace rubbed his forehead with a handkerchief, sweating a little from the exertion and still catching his breath. "I was coming to find the inspector. I found the weapon used on the sergeant – well, at least I think it is. A huge chunk of wood splintered and bloodstained. Whoever walloped him must have tossed it over the hedge."

"That was rather clumsy of them," said Marjorie.

"I thought so too. I expect they were disturbed. It wouldn't surprise me if they were going to go back for it once this hullabaloo died down. I'd better let the DI or Frankie know where it is before they get the chance."

"Let the DI know what?" Patricia Bloom had recovered her sense of calm, giving Marjorie a bashful smile. "Sorry about earlier. It's been a long day."

"Think nothing of it," said Marjorie. "But we need to talk. Edna has a confession, Horace has some news, and I may have discovered something that might be of help to you in your investigation."

DI Bloom blew out a heavy sigh, looking around the room. "There are still several people we've got to get through. I'd appreciate it if you could keep it brief."

Horace spoke first. "I've found what I think could be the weapon used to attack your sergeant."

"Where?"

"It's behind a large laurel to the west of the grounds."

A police van drew up outside with a few more officers and a forensics team. "About time too," muttered DI Bloom. "Come with me," she said to Horace while hurrying down the steps. Marjorie and Edna were left standing in the foyer.

"It looks as though she might be some time. Shall we go in search of Frederick?" Marjorie suggested.

Edna shrugged. "Might as well."

On descending the steps, Marjorie overheard DI Bloom directing the forensics team to the spot where Frankie had left a cordon. She then told another officer to accompany her as she set off with Horace in search of the weapon. Frankie appeared, looking upset and dishevelled.

"Where the hell have you been?" Patricia Bloom snapped, but didn't give him time to answer. "Never mind now. Get inside and help Mahoney with the interviews. You two go too," she fired the order over her shoulder as she hurried after Horace.

"Are you sure I should mention the papers?" Edna appeared unusually worried.

"Don't tell me you're frightened of the dear inspector."

Edna stiffened. "Not exactly, but she's a bit volatile, ain't she?"

Like someone else I know, thought Marjorie. "You've met your match, then?"

"I just don't want to spend the night in a prison cell, if it's okay with you," Edna retorted. "Besides, it won't help. The papers are gone."

"We just have to hope that whoever stole them hasn't had time to destroy them. They may hold the answer to this whole nasty business."

"And they might not."

"What did you find out from the Stewarts, by the way?" Marjorie listened to Edna as they walked around the side of the hotel where she and Grace had been earlier.

Edna told her about the camping trip where the children had seen Jock's father leaving the farmhouse on the same night a couple died.

"Grace told me the same story. She was there too; it seems Jock couldn't believe his father carried out the crime that night. Then there was the sheep rustling that was the final straw, resulting in McGuire senior taking his own life. Grace believes, as did the authorities, that guilt over the death of the couple in the farmhouse caused him to commit suicide. She also thinks for reasons unknown that the sergeant may have murdered Jock."

"That's a long stretch. Terry Stewart said his wife told him the sergeant and Jock were friends once and they fell out, but I don't see why he would murder him," said Edna.

"I agree with you. When we connect what happened to that couple with what Jock was going to write in his book, we may know why he was killed. I can't believe it was over some sin carried out years ago by any of our suspects, but we can't rule it out. It's so frustrating; we really need that manuscript."

"Maybe the sin is more recent," said Edna.

"It could be," said Marjorie, thinking of Grace's affair with Bill, but she couldn't really believe either of them would have killed over that if Grace was being honest when she said her husband wouldn't care.

"Gemma let slip Sergeant Bell had hooked up with someone, but she wouldn't say who. Can you imagine anyone falling for him? Either way, if it's a secret, you can bet their spouses don't know."

"That's interesting," said Marjorie. For some reason she felt the desire to protect Grace from Edna's wrath. Edna would show no mercy if she discovered *the blonde* was having an extramarital affair, and she had no desire to give her cousin-in-law unnecessary ammunition nor to burst Frederick and Horace's bubbles unless it became necessary.

"I doubt that fact has anything to do with tonight's attack. Unless..." Edna stopped walking and looked down at Marjorie.

"What?"

"Maybe it was one of the spouses that attacked Bell and it's separate from Jock's murder. That would make much more sense 'cos I can't see why McGuire's killer would attack a policeman."

Before Marjorie could reply, they saw Frederick heading towards them, a huge grin on his face. "Thank God you're safe," he said.

Chapter 30

Marjorie was lost for a moment in the affection shown by Frederick for her wellbeing, and it took her a few minutes to compose herself. Thankfully, Edna made it clear she was freezing cold and frogmarched them back to the hotel, oblivious to the almost paused unspoken interaction between herself and Frederick.

Really, Marjorie Snellthorpe! You must get a hold of yourself. You're behaving like a besotted youth. After giving herself a stern talking to on the way back, reality struck when they rejoined the guests being interviewed in the lounge. There were even fewer people than when they had left with four police officers, including Frankie, now taking statements. Frankie's eyes darting backwards and forwards and his agitated demeanour gave the impression he wanted to be anywhere but in the room. Perhaps he was having second thoughts about his chosen line of work.

Grace was at the bar being consoled by Mick Burns — who may have become her second confidante — with a glass in her hand. With blurry eyes, it was difficult to tell whether she was still upset about Bill Bell, or just plain drunk. She wobbled on the stool. Mick reached out a hand to stop her from falling and Marjorie decided it was the latter.

"Where's Horace?" Edna interrupted her thinking.

"I left him outside," said Frederick.

"No. We've seen him since then," snapped Edna, as if Frederick should have known all that happened while he was out of sight. "He went off with that moody DI to find the weapon."

"Do you mean the weapon that was used in the attack?" Frederick asked.

"What other weapon would I mean? Keep up, Fred. How many attacks have you witnessed tonight?"

"Now just a minute…" Frederick began, but decided there was little use arguing with Edna once she was on a roll.

"He found a lump of bloodstained wood over the hedge off the side of the terrace. He and DI Bloom and another police officer – from forensics, I think – left before Edna and I came looking for you." Marjorie explained.

"Did you tell her about our room search?" Frederick cast a resentful glance Edna's way.

Marjorie was in no doubt Frederick regretted rooting through a room he had no business being in.

"I'm afraid we didn't get the opportunity. Let's grab ourselves a hot toddy and discuss our suspects while we wait."

"Good idea," said Edna. "I'm parched. All this searching for you lot has worn me out."

Marjorie held a finger to her lips, advising Frederick to ignore her cousin-in-law.

Brian appeared and took their drinks order. Frederick lowered his voice. "Why haven't we spoken to him and Nessa?"

"Because I can't believe Nessa had anything to do with Jock McGuire's death or the attack tonight."

Edna leaned in. "Why?"

"It's bad for business. Nessa's not stupid. She and Brian would have known McGuire planned to check out this morning, and I don't believe he had anything to write about her that would give her – and by that same reasoning, Brian – a motive for murder. It's definitely not Grace either. I don't believe she had anything to do with it."

"Pity," said Edna. "And if it wasn't the sergeant, it leaves Mick or Gemma Stewart in the frame."

"It could have been Mick," said Frederick. "He was close to the scene both times. He wouldn't talk to me, by the way. If it was him, he didn't mean for his daughter to stumble upon the body. They had told him they were having an early night. Probably going off for a secret stroll without telling him."

"I don't think it was Gemma. Like Marjorie says, she doesn't have enough of a motive. Other than an affair with Mick years ago, which her husband knew about. That brings us back to Mick because his daughter is ignorant of the fact. I suppose it could have been Terry protecting her honour, like. Although I don't know why he'd have clobbered the sergeant. Although he said he overheard Frankie telling the DI, Bell knew who the killer was. He

235

might have been trying to throw us off his scent, though. I think they're separate crimes and it was a jealous spouse got to him."

Frederick's forehead creased.

Marjorie explained what they had discovered so far about Sergeant Bell having an affair with someone, but continued to withhold who it was with. Edna took over and told him about the farmhouse killings from when the suspects were all teenagers and how Jock's father was the person most likely responsible.

"Terry told us Gemma said there was someone else there that night. For all we know, it could have been Jock."

"Edna! You're a genius! That's it. It's been staring us in the face all along – well, not quite all along – but I think I know who that other person was. DI Bloom needs to pull the case files from the farmhouse murders and we'll identify the killer."

"Jock!" said Edna.

Marjorie couldn't help chortling. "Now it's you who needs to keep up. He hardly hit himself over the head with a rock, did he? And unless he came back from the dead, he didn't attack Sergeant Bell."

Edna's face went a bright shade of pink. "But you just said I was a genius."

"And so you are, my dear. It's all about the other man who was in the car that night."

"I think I'm following you," said Frederick.

"Bully for you," said Edna. "Personally, I think she's lost her marbles again."

"We must find DI Bloom and prevent another murder," said Marjorie.

Chapter 31

Marjorie's heart was beating so fast she thought it might explode. DI Bloom burst into the hotel, rubbing her hands and stamping her feet, trying to shake off the cold. She summoned the other officers, who had just about finished with their interviews, and commandeered Nessa's office. Brian took them a tray of hot drinks and came out of the office shaking his head.

"Why do they nae have their meetings at the pub in the village? It does nae do us any good having them roond here."

Nessa sat on a sofa in the lobby. For the first time since Marjorie had met her, she looked defeated. "They have a job to do, Brian. And so do we."

"Aye, if they dinnae scare all the guests away. They'll all be checking oot in the morning."

Faith joined Nessa on the sofa, patting her arm. "Everything will work out. As soon as the police find who's responsible for all this," she waved her arm around, "everyone will forget about it."

Nessa rubbed her forehead with both hands, eyes filling up. "Do you think so?"

"Absolutely," said Faith. "Most of your guests come from out of the area. There might be a few comments on social media, but sometimes things like this actually attract visitors, rather than deter them."

"She's right," said Brian, realising he'd upset his charge. "We'll get through it. Most of the guests have gone to bed now. Ignore me, I just dinnae like having the police aboot blethering, that's all."

Faith caught Marjorie's eye and called her over. "It hasn't put you off the hotel, has it, Marjorie?"

"Not at all," said Marjorie. Taking the mantle, she added, "We were just saying we haven't had this much excitement in years, weren't we?"

Edna and Frederick shuffled over to where Nessa and Faith were sitting.

"Yeah," said Edna. "Beats going to the cinema any day."

Nessa gave an unconvinced smile. "I'm not so sure, but thank you for your support."

The quintet chatted for around half an hour and by the end of it Nessa was looking much more like the exuberant hostess they had met when they first arrived. Marjorie was itching to ask her about the farmhouse murders and what she remembered of that night, but couldn't bring herself to. Edna, however, had no such misgivings.

"Gemma Stewart was telling me and Horace earlier how you witnessed a robbery when you were kids. Seems people round these parts aren't strangers to murder, are they?"

Nessa paled again, and from her fidgeting, Marjorie feared she might run. Instead, she stared into space as if recalling distant memories. "You're referring to the farmhouse murders."

Faith gawped at Nessa. "What happened?"

"A couple died. It was years ago. Brian knows more about it than I do. He and dad went to the farm after the bodies of a couple were found." Nessa stared up at Brian.

"Aye. They were toonsers, bought the farmhouse, and were going to convert it into a luxury complex. People roond here were nae happy aboot it. Word got around they had money, and Paddy McGuire went and robbed the place."

Marjorie scrunched her eyes, confused. "Toonsers?"

"From the city," explained Frederick.

"I see. Do you believe Mr McGuire killed the couple?" Marjorie asked.

"The kids saw him leaving the farmhouse that night all right. Someone had bashed the guy who died over the head, just like Phil. His wife must have heard something, and the police said she died after falling down the stairs." Brian closed his eyes for a moment. "It was nae a pretty sight. Me and Craig – Nessa's dad – were on the way to work when we saw the wee lass who did their cleaning, running down the road. The wee laddie was just sat there when we got inside, pale as anything. There was nothing we could do. Craig went back to the village to get Eddie – the local copper at the time – he dealt with it after that."

Nessa shook her head. "Paddy McGuire should have been prosecuted, but none of us could swear it was him getting into the car that night. It was so dark. The Sheriff's office decided there wasn't enough evidence. When we saw the car, we thought it was just Paddy up to his tricks; he was always arguing with someone."

"Like his son," said Edna.

"If we're being honest, most people in the village were glad to see the back of them. Not in the way they died right enough, but they didn't want the countryside dogged by some big posh mansion sticking out like a sore thumb," Brian explained.

"Gemma suggested someone else was in the car with Jock erm… Phil's father. Did you see anyone?" Marjorie asked.

Nessa shook her head unconvincingly. Convinced this tryst between her and the others was the key to the whole thing, yet it was turning out to be the hardest to break down. They were protecting someone. Marjorie saw Grace and Mick had stopped talking and were sidling over to where they sat. Everyone else had disappeared. The time had come to crack open the lies.

"With one man dead and another as good as dead, I think it's time to stop covering up for him or her, isn't it?"

"What does she mean?" Brian demanded.

"Yes. I'd like to know too." DI Patricia Bloom had suddenly appeared behind Marjorie and perched herself on the arm of her chair. Frankie stood next to her.

"There's no cover-up here, Lady Marjorie," Grace interrupted before addressing the inspector. "Shouldn't you be finding out who attacked Bill Bell?"

If she was stunned by the antagonistic way in which Grace addressed her, Patricia Bloom hid it well. "Mrs Wallace. Do you have anything to tell me?"

Nessa looked at Grace's pleading eyes before saying quietly. "No, sorry. Now. I have a hotel to run, so if you'll excuse me." Nessa shot off to her office with Brian in hot pursuit.

"What about you, Mrs Brown-Jones?" Marjorie admired DI Bloom's tenacity.

"There's nothing to say. I need to go." Grace Brown-Jones scurried towards the exit, albeit in a slightly more dignified way than the hotel proprietor.

"I'll go after her," said Frankie. "We haven't interviewed her about tonight yet."

"Well, don't be long. I need you here."

"Have you finished with us, ma'am?" One of the officers asked.

"Yes. You'd better get back to Inverness's Sunday night crime scenes."

Once they left, Patricia Bloom fixed her eyes on Marjorie's. "What's going on?"

"I'm not entirely sure, but I believe Jock McGuire was going to reveal – or at least postulate – the name of the person some people saw with his father on the night of an aggravated robbery which ended up with two people dying decades ago."

"The farmhouse murders. A few people have mentioned that tonight in relation to Jock's father's suicide. One even thought it might have been a motive for

Jock McGuire's murder, but I don't see how that has anything to do with Sergeant Bell's death."

"He's died then?" Marjorie asked.

"Yes. I just got the call ten minutes ago, but no-one else knows. I need the team focussed."

"Good," said Marjorie. "Sorry. I didn't mean good about the sergeant's death, I meant good no-one else knows. You see, I think believing he's still alive might come in handy."

Patricia Bloom took what Marjorie was saying in her stride, unlike Edna.

"You're talking in riddles again, Marge. What's this all about?"

"Marjorie believes the second man in the car that night was Sergeant Bell," Frederick suggested.

"Yes I do. Obviously he wasn't a police officer then, just a teenager who – I expect – found himself bedazzled by one Paddy McGuire, Jock's father. I'm almost certain he was the now Grace Brown-Jones's boyfriend. Hence the conspiracy of silence. The four people who witnessed Paddy McGuire getting into that car have been protecting him for decades."

Patricia Bloom said nothing. "He's been volunteering to work in these parts a lot of late. He was nasty, and a bit of a prat, but I didn't have him down as a killer."

"Me neither, and he obviously didn't kill himself either," said Marjorie. "Nevertheless, I feel in order to find out who the killer is, we – rather you – need to pull the files of the earlier crime."

"I'm confused. Who did kill them?" Edna's eyes were bulging. Patience never being a strong suit. "I bet it was Mick Burns. Self-righteous so and so. Or *the blonde*," she added for effect, glaring at Frederick. "By the way, where's Horace?"

"Oh, do try to stick to the point," said Marjorie. "It was certainly not Grace Brown-Jones."

"How do you know that?" Edna snapped.

"I just do. And I don't think it was Mick, although it's possible. Look, Inspector. Do you think you could find out about the boy?"

"What boy?" Edna huffed.

"The five-year-old who sat up all night with his dead parents and was left scarred for life."

"Now I get you," said Patricia. "Give me ten minutes."

Ten minutes later there was a hushed discussion as Patricia Bloom revealed what she had discovered. Towards the end of the discussion Frankie arrived back with Grace, who headed for the stairs.

"Frankie," Patricia barked. "Get Mr Burns and Mr and Mrs Stewart down here, then meet us in Mrs Wallace's office."

Marjorie heaved a sigh of relief the inspector didn't call Grace back. It would be too much for her. "Are you sure this will work, Marge?" Edna asked.

Horace appeared from nowhere when they were about to go into Nessa's office.

"Where have you been?" Edna snapped before noticing a bandage over his head. "What happened?"

"I tripped over in the garden and hit my head on a stone sculpture. One of the staff was just leaving and gave me a lift to the village where the local doctor patched me up. Just a few stitches. No harm done. What's happening here?"

"We'll tell you in a minute," said Edna, taking his arm.

Once everyone was assembled in Nessa's office, DI Bloom put on an Oscar-winning performance. "I have some good news for you all," she began. "Sergeant Bell is out of danger; he's had surgery to remove a clot on his brain and is in recovery. He should be awake enough in the morning for me to interview him, and then I think we can put this whole thing to bed. I'll leave a uniformed officer here, so don't anyone try to leave without my express permission. Frankie, you can tell Mahoney he's got the short straw."

"Yes, ma'am. Great news about Bill."

Marjorie pulled DI Bloom to one side once everyone else had left. "There's still another person in danger tonight," she said.

"I understand. I'll make a pretence to leave and park my car in the village."

"How will you get back?"

"I'll walk. It's only a couple of miles. In the meantime, I'll leave her with you awesome foursome," she smirked. "I heard the name from Faith Weathers. She told me while I was interviewing her I should listen to you. I hear you have quite a past."

Marjorie chuckled. "I wouldn't quite say that."

"Anyway, please keep the woman with you until I get back. Mahoney will be out front if you need him."

"And who will be at the hospital?"

"Don't worry about that end. It's all sorted. There's always a chance our killer didn't swallow the bait."

"Oh, I think they have. It's just a matter of which person they go for first." Marjorie caught up with the others and explained they were on babysitting duty for a while.

Chapter 32

Grace Brown-Jones took some convincing to let them into her room. Her eyes were still swollen, and she was wearing a towelling bathrobe and a face mask. Once inside, Marjorie explained what they were doing there. Grace was aghast at hearing her life might be in danger.

"I've never heard anything so ridiculous in all my life."

"You've got nothing to lose by letting us stay. If we're wrong, it will have been a mild inconvenience, but if we're right… well, it goes without saying, you'll be grateful."

Grace sucked in her lips before acquiescing.

"Good," said Horace. "I suggest that if we hear anything, we come into your bedroom and hide in the wardrobe. And if we don't, we'll sit quietly in the sitting room while you sleep."

"Your expansive sitting room, or your expansive wardrobe." Edna couldn't resist a dig at the size of Grace's accommodation. She hadn't stopped tutting since they were reluctantly allowed inside.

Ignoring or not understanding the dart, Grace snapped. "I'm hardly going to sleep, am I? What, with you lot in my sitting room and someone intent on killing me!"

"But you must pretend to, my dear," said Marjorie, "or the killer of Jock McGuire and, I'm afraid, Sergeant Bell will get away with murder."

"Is Bill…?"

"I'm afraid so."

Grace's protestations ended there, and she did as requested, going into her bedroom and at least making a pretence at going to bed.

"Shouldn't one of us be in there with her?" asked Horace.

Marjorie raised a hand when she saw Edna's mouth open, no doubt to say something rude. "The window will be locked. The killer – if they come at all – will walk through that door. I just hope the inspector makes it back before anything happens."

"Don't you worry, Marjorie. Fred and I can handle this, eh, Fred?"

Frederick looked less convinced than Horace, but gave a weak smile-cum-grimace. "Of course."

"I'm stronger than the pair of you," said Edna. "No-one's getting killed on my watch."

Marjorie agreed with her cousin-in-law. She felt Horace and Edna would stand a better chance against any intruder than Horace and Frederick. "Let's hope none of our services will be required, but perhaps Edna should join Horace in the wardrobe if they are."

Fighting to stay awake and with no sign of DI Bloom, Marjorie noticed a light from Horace's watch.

"What time is it?" she whispered.

"Two-thirty. I wonder what's keeping the inspector?"

"Shush!" Frederick. They heard the unmistakeable creak of floorboards outside.

"Time to move," hissed Horace. "You and Fred hide in the bathroom, Marjorie. Edna and I will take the wardrobe, as you suggested."

Grace's voice sounded frightened as they opened the door and snuck into her bedroom. "Is this it?"

"Yes," said Horace, sounding almost excited. "Don't you worry, just stay still. We need to catch our night stalker in the act."

Horace and Edna squashed themselves inside the wardrobe, leaving a small crack. Marjorie and Frederick were just behind the bathroom door when they heard footsteps tiptoeing across the sitting room towards the bedroom. The door slowly opened and the shadow of a person dressed in black paused, listening. Grace delivered a pretend snore, which satisfied the intruder. They crossed the carpeted floor. Just as the trespasser lifted something heavy, the light switch was flicked on from behind. DI Bloom and PC Mahoney were on the man in an instant. It was perhaps as well because somehow Edna and Horace had managed to pull the wardrobe door too far and shut themselves inside. Marjorie couldn't get past Frederick, who was hyperventilating, so all in all, they would have been of no use had the police not got there first. By the time Marjorie and Frederick got out of the bedroom and let the embarrassed couple out of the wardrobe, the scuffle on the floor ended with the assailant in handcuffs. DI

Bloom removed the balaclava from Frankie Charles's head.

"Idiot," she said. "You're nicked. Read him his rights, Mahoney."

"Frank Charles, I'm arresting you for the murder of Jock McGuire and Bill Bell—"

"You said he was still alive!" Frankie yelled at Patricia Bloom.

DI Bloom shrugged, "Continue, PC Mahoney."

PC Mahoney did as instructed and Frankie glared at Grace. "You protected a monster for all these years."

Much more together now her would-be murderer was in cuffs, Grace glowered at the young man. "Bill wasn't a monster. He was an easily led teenager, manipulated and groomed by Paddy McGuire to follow where he led. Bill was in the sitting room that night, rifling through drawers when the 'have-a-go hero' went for McGuire. He told me they fought, and the man fell backwards and hit his head. The woman came out screaming and fell down the stairs. Paddy and Bill ran away. It was a tragic accident. I only heard tonight there was a child. I'm sorry for your loss, but it was not murder."

"It was no accident. Not from where I was kneeling on the landing. He lied to you. I saw it all. Paddy McGuire – I didn't know that's who he was at the time – picked up a poker and whacked my da over the head. I cried out, and my ma ran out. She tried to hide the scene from me and fell backwards down the stairs. I can still hear her scream. That monster Paddy did not try to help either of them. He yelled at the youth to get out of there. I never saw who he was. I only found out when Jock McGuire came up here. He was going to use his book to convince everyone his da was innocent. I couldn't have that."

"But no-one would have believed it. The case was closed," said DI Bloom. "The Sheriff took his suicide as an admission of guilt and with the statements taken from the teenagers that night, although not strong enough evidence to convict, it was obvious Paddy McGuire was the person who entered your parents' farmhouse. You must have read the file?"

"I still had to stop him publishing."

"And stop him you did," said Marjorie. "Did he see you on the day we arrived?"

"Yeah. He must have recognised me. I'm the spitting image of my dad, so my adoptive parents always told me. I don't have any photos 'cos *she* burnt everything when she knocked the farmhouse down."

All eyes turned towards Grace. "I bought the property from a trust and turned it into pastureland for the stags. It hadn't been touched since they found the bodies." She looked with pleading eyes at Frankie. "I swear, I didn't know there was a child, but I still don't believe for one minute that Bill lied to me." Her eyes blazed as they filled with tears. "It was just a stupid book. Jock… Phil McGuire was going to make sure we were all in it. He had some misguided belief that the book would destroy us, but it wouldn't have. There might have been a few turned heads, and he'd have sold a dozen copies and, before long, everyone would have forgotten about it. We'd have ridden the storm. There was no need to kill him."

"I found out Jock was going to say my dad attacked his dad that night, and not the other way around." Frankie's eyes blazed in return.

"When did you find out Sergeant Bell was the other person?" Marjorie asked.

"When I found papers after we searched McGuire's room. There was a letter from Jock telling Bell he was going to be named in the book. Someone must have talked. Nessa I expect."

"Your adoptive mother," Marjorie stated.

"How did you know?"

"The way she looked at you and the way you rebuffed her this afternoon. I couldn't work it out at the time, but since then, it clicked into place. She's carried the guilt of knowing who the other man was, for years, trying to protect her friend." Marjorie glanced at Grace. "Your mother has a conscience."

"I'll never forgive her for hiding that man's identity from me. Not that we were ever close. I stayed with my da."

"Nessa's ex," Marjorie explained to the confused-looking onlookers. "She hid it from you because, no doubt, the reason you didn't get on is that she sensed your anger and feared what you might do with the knowledge."

"Then why tell McGuire about Bill?" Grace asked.

"I doubt she did," said Marjorie. "It's far more likely he worked it out for himself, or Bill himself told him when they were still friends. Offloading his guilt."

"Nessa had adopted you?" Grace's eyes filled with confusion. "I heard she had an estranged child, but didn't know it was through adoption or that it was the son of the farmhouse couple."

"Brian would have kept the fact they found a young child at the scene secret. What a cruel twist of fate that your adoptive mother was one of the very people who witnessed some of the goings-on from that night," said Marjorie.

Frankie gave a cynical laugh. "You could call it that. Once I found out from my da – he was like a real da to me – that my so-called mother and I were both from Scraghead and she had witnessed what happened, I moved to Inverness. I wanted to be closer to where my real parents died. After a while, I was determined to know who else was in the car that night."

"You wanted revenge," said Marjorie.

"Aye. I did. Wouldn't you?" Frankie yelled. "I dragged Bill outside after we searched the room and challenged him aboot what was in those papers upstairs. You know what he did? He laughed in my face, told me to forget it. That the book had most likely been burned, and he was innocent."

"Well he was," Grace sobbed. "He didn't kill your parents."

"No. You're right there. He just stole the watch my da was wearing. I didn't see his face, but I saw what he did."

"The Rolex? He told me it was a gift from his granddad."

"Check my pocket," he said. "It was a wedding present from my mam."

"Did he know you were the man's son?" DI Bloom asked.

"Not until he lay on the ground, pleading and groaning like a baby. Then he knew. I thought he was dead, but I didn't get a chance to make sure. I heard a couple come out onto the terrace."

"I'm sorry for what happened to you all those years ago, Frankie, but you still killed two men in cold blood. You're no better than they were. If you really wanted justice, you could have gone after evidence," said Marjorie. "And tonight you were going to kill again. And who knows? Brian and Nessa could have been next on your list. Once you started down this road, there was no going back, was there?"

"They deserved to die. They all do." Rage filled Frankie's eyes and face. He struggled to free his hands from behind his back as he glared at Grace. "You're as bad as he was. You'll get what's coming to you."

"I think it's time we left," said Patricia Bloom, giving PC Mahoney a nod.

Mahoney led the struggling Frankie out of the room and another PC arrived to help. DI Bloom turned to

Marjorie and the others. "It seems Faith Weathers was right. You really are the awesome foursome." She winked.

Chapter 33

The next morning, the restaurant was buzzing with energy. The guests knew the murderer had been arrested, and they were free to enjoy the rest of their holiday. In fact, people were brimming over with enthusiasm and support for Nessa and her venture.

Nessa was back to her ebullient self, except for a slight sadness in the eyes Marjorie detected. Otherwise, she was chatting with everyone as she floated around the restaurant.

It was only the awesome foursome, as they had come to be known, that were slightly subdued. Even Edna said she felt sorry for Frankie.

"Imagine witnessing your parent dying like that at five years old. I don't think I could forgive either."

"There's a difference between forgiveness and downright malice, though, isn't there. As I said last night, once he started killing, it wouldn't have stopped. The rest of those, unfortunate enough to have witnessed the two men driving away, I'm sure were next on his list. You see, he chose the darkest of paths and no matter how many people he killed, he could never find peace through revenge. Nessa recognised the evil in him. I expect it was one reason for the marriage breakup. Only forgiveness brings release in the end."

"Marjorie's right, Edna," said Horace. "The lad deserves to go to prison for the rest of his life. There can be no excuse for cold-blooded murder. Remember, he was also going to kill Grace."

"Oh yes. I wondered how long it would be before you brought up *the blonde*," said Edna.

"Now, now, Edna. Jealousy doesn't become you," said Horace.

Ignoring him, Edna said, "I'm just pleased the monster had nothing to do with it." Glaring at Frederick who had opened his mouth to speak, she added, "And before any of you say anything; it don't mean the wretched thing doesn't exist."

Marjorie was pleased Edna's irrational fear that the Loch Ness Monster had anything to do with the disastrous events had not been realised, but it was clear the phobia hadn't entirely gone away.

"I was going to say that while I feel sorry for the policeman's childhood experience," said Frederick. "I can't agree with what he did."

Faith, Nessa, and Grace approached their table before an argument developed.

"I owe you all immense gratitude for what you did," said Nessa. "You not only saved my friend's life, but most likely my hotel. I'm sad about Frankie, but he chose the wrong path." Nessa dabbed away the moisture from the corners of her eyes.

"Yes, thanks," said Grace. "Sorry I didn't believe you."

"They're awesome, that's for sure," said Faith. "You did it again, Marjorie,"

Edna huffed. "*We...* We did it again."

"Of course," said Faith.

"Don't mention it," said Marjorie. "Anyway, I'd much rather talk about how a certain two people managed to lock themselves inside a wardrobe."

Guffaws all round, including joint snorts from Edna and Horace, dispelled the mood that had been about to descend upon the quartet.

THE END

Author's Note

Thank you for reading *Murder in the Highlands*, the second book in the Lady Marjorie Snellthorpe series. If you have enjoyed it, please leave an honest review any platform you may use.

If you would like to read the prequel to the series, the novella *Death of a Blogger* is available for free when you sign up for my newsletter where you will receive news and offers once a month. If you prefer not to subscribe to newsletters, the book is available to purchase from most eBook stores, or to borrow, on request, from libraries. Print and audiobook versions are also available.

To find out what happens to our feisty pensioners next keep an eye on my website at *www.dawnbrookespublishing.com*.

Discover where the Lady Marjorie character began; check out the Rachel Prince Mystery series.

Books by Dawn Brookes

Lady Marjorie Snellthorpe Mysteries

Death of a Blogger (prequel novella)
Murder at the Opera House
Murder in the Highlands
Murder at a Wimbledon Mansion (coming soon)

Rachel Prince Mysteries

A Cruise to Murder
Deadly Cruise
Killer Cruise
Dying to Cruise
A Christmas Cruise Murder
Murderous Cruise Habit
Honeymoon Cruise Murder
A Murder Mystery Cruise
Hazardous Cruise
Captain's Dinner Cruise Murder
Corporate Cruise Murder (Available to preorder)

Carlos Jacobi PI

Body in the Woods
The Bradgate Park Murders
Body at the Jewry Wall (coming soon)

Memoirs

Hurry up Nurse: Memoirs of nurse training in the 1970s
Hurry up Nurse 2: London calling
Hurry up Nurse 3: More adventures in the life of a student nurse

Picture Books for Children

Ava & Oliver's Bonfire Night Adventure
Ava & Oliver's Christmas Nativity Adventure
Danny the Caterpillar
Gerry the One-Eared Cat
Suki Seal and the Plastic Ring

Keep in touch:

Sign up for my no-spam newsletter at:
www.dawnbrookespublishing.com

Follow me on Facebook:
www.facebook.com/dawnbrookespublishing/

Follow me on TikTok
tiktok.com/@dawnbrookesauthor

Follow me on YouTube:
www.youtube.com/c/DawnBrookesPublishing

Acknowledgements

Thank you to my scrutiny team for the suggestions and amendments, making the finished version a more polished read. Thanks to Alex Davis for proofreading the final document.

Thanks to my immediate circle of friends who are so patient with me when I'm absorbed in my fictional world and for your continued support in all my endeavours.

Thank you so much to my Advance Reader Team for comments and support.

About the Author

Award winning author Dawn Brookes is author of the *Rachel Prince Mystery* series, combining a unique blend of murder, cruising and medicine with a touch of romance. She is also author of the Carlos Jacobi crime series and the Lady Marjorie Snellthorpe Mystery series.

Dawn holds an MA in Creative Writing with Distinction and has a 39-year nursing pedigree. She loves to travel and takes regular cruise holidays, which she says are for research purposes! She brings these passions and a love of clean crime to her writing.

The surname of her Rachel Prince protagonist is in honour of her childhood dog, Prince, who used to put his head on her knee while she lost herself in books.

Author of *Hurry up Nurse: memoirs of nurse training in the 1970s* and *Hurry up Nurse 2: London calling*, Dawn worked as a hospital nurse, midwife, district nurse and community matron across her career. Before turning her hand to writing for a living, she had multiple articles published in professional journals and coedited a nursing textbook.

She grew up in Leicester, later moved to London and

Berkshire, but now lives in Derbyshire. Dawn holds a Bachelor's degree with Honours and a Master's degree in education. Writing across genres, she also writes for children. Dawn has a passion for nature and loves animals, especially dogs. Animals will continue to feature in her children's books, as she believes caring for animals and nature helps children to become kinder human beings.

Made in United States
Orlando, FL
09 August 2022